Secret of the

Purloined
Bracelet

Secret of the Purloined Bracelet

Hidden Truths Vol. 4

Wendy VanHatten

DocUmeant *Publishing*
244 5th Avenue
Suite G-200
NY, NY 10001
646-233-4366
www.DocUmeantPublishing.com

Secret of the Purloined Bracelet

Hidden Truths Series, Vol. 4

Published byDocUmeant Publishing 244 5th Avenue, Suite G-200 NY, NY 10001

Phone: 646-233-4366

Copy Editor JoAnn Rasmussen

Cover Design and Layout Ginger Marks

DocUmeantDesigns.com

Printed in The United States of America

ISBN13: 978-1-937801-61-8
ISBN10: 1-937801-61-6

Prologue

"Tonight's the night. You have the codes, the list, and your instructions. Remember, the old man doesn't live. Got it?" The caller's barked-out instructions made him jump back. "Don't screw this up or you'll wish I didn't know where you live. Are. We. Clear?" The phone almost jumped out of his hand as the voice came through loud and menacing.

"Yeah, yeah. I got . . ." He didn't get to finish his sentence as the caller had hung up.

Chapter 1

"What the hell are these, Shadow?" Taking a bigger than normal drink of her Prosecco, Marta choked and coughed. "How on earth did I miss them? I could have sworn I looked at this one before now." Carefully, she checked the back of the journal-like diary to see if there were any more. Satisfied this was all, she gingerly arranged the few yellowed, black and white photos she pulled out of the back of one of her grandma's old journals. "After the last two years, I seriously hoped I was done with surprises. Finished. But, I guess not. Let's see what we have, Shadow." Her fluffy, Maine Coon cat jumped off her lap and began another nightly grooming of his six-inch whiskers.

"Grandma, did you stuff these in the back cover and forget about them? Oh, how I wish you were alive so I could ask you about these." Marta looked toward the heavens and then gently tried to smooth out the creased photos, being careful not to tear them. Picking up one, she could tell it was the tiara her grandma left to her. That was obvious. When Marta found that, the museum curator and historian here in Venice knew exactly what it was. It was from a royal family who ruled here hundreds of years ago. Unbeknownst to Marta, her grandmother was part of that family. Marta laid the photo of the tiara aside and picked up the next one.

There were two photos of necklaces. "These pictures are both so wrinkled and discolored; it's kind of hard to tell if there's a difference in the pieces. Are they the same necklace or two different ones? I really think they're different, but I only have one necklace from Grandma. Where do you suppose the other one is, Shadow? Since, there's no date on any of these, I have no idea when they were taken. I'll bet it was at least fifty years ago, though. But, why just take a picture of the jewelry and whoever was wearing it?" Shadow looked at Marta and then went back to grooming, apparently not concerned.

Lastly, there were two photos of bracelets. "Grandma . . . bracelets?" As Marta looked more closely at one of the wrinkled photos, she gasped. "Wait a minute. I've seen this one before. Where's my phone?"

Pulling up the email and photo she recently received from George Hanson in San Francisco, Marta compared it to the old photo in front of her. "This is the same bracelet. I'd bet a month of cat treats and Prosecco on that, Shadow." At the mention of treats, Shadow meowed and walked toward the cupboard where the treats were kept. "Okay, you can have a couple. Then, I'm calling Mario to see if we can use his plane. It's a good thing your shots are up to date. We have to get to San Francisco. Now."

Chapter 2

"You sure he's not gonna hear us?" The whisper sounded loud to both men in the eerily quiet, darkened house.

"Yep. I got a good source who told me the old man goes to bed at nine o'clock every night after drinking two glasses of wine. It's midnight. He won't hear a thing. Besides, this is the night my guy told me is the best. Otherwise, we'd have to wait a couple of weeks. And, that won't work."

"Yeah, but what if he didn't this time? What if he's waiting for us? What if something goes wrong? Things could be bad. Real bad." The whisper became slightly louder, the whisperer more agitated.

"Stop worrying. Stop talking. And follow me. Do exactly like we planned, and we can get out of here with everything. Got your gloves on? And, your face mask?"

The whisperer nodded in the dark. Then, he couldn't help himself. "Franco, how are we going to get all the wine and the paintings into the car? Why are we taking wine, anyway? Can't he buy his own?"

"For Pete's sake . . . we've gone over all of this a million times. Pay attention and follow me. And, for the last time . . . shut up."

The whisperer nodded, wishing he were a cat so he could see something, anything, in the shadow-filled hallway. Thoughts filled his head as he followed Franco's small light down the long hall to the right of the grand foyer, but he didn't say another word. After all, things were going just the way Franco said they would. He just hoped they could find the right wine and the paintings and get out of here quickly. When they delivered it all, they would be rich. He had shivers thinking about all the money he would have. Then he wouldn't have to sneak around anymore, breaking into houses, and stealing things. He was due to have some good luck. He couldn't wait.

But, right now this place was beginning to give him the creeps. Shapes appeared in the dark, and he almost tripped over a chair. "Cripes! Who puts a chair in the hallway, anyway?" The whisper came out louder than he intended, and Franco turned and clamped a gloved hand over his mouth.

"I told you to shut up." Franco hissed in his face and then removed his hand.

"Stop with the lecture. Who's going to hear us anyway? You said he was asleep." The whisperer moved away from Franco, his thoughts swirling around in his head. I'm not stupid. Why is Franco treating me like a two year old, especially when my friend and I introduced him to Bart in Venice? He should be nicer to me. When I get my share of the money, I'll tell him where to go. He smiled as he thought of having piles of money.

Franco stopped in front of a door. "Pay attention. I'm going to unlock this door to the wine cellar using the code my source gave me. Then, I'll grab only the wine on this list. It will all be on shelves along the left wall, at the bottom. I know exactly where it is. While I'm doing that, you rearrange a few bottles like we talked so it's not noticeable right away any bottles are missing. Be careful with the bottles. Don't wipe off any dust or make any noise when you move the bottles. It's just like we planned. Got it?"

"Got it. Where did you say the paintings were?" The whisperer looked over his shoulder, down the dark hallway.

Using his penlight, Franco concentrated on entering numbers on the keypad and didn't answer him. With the last number entered, the door made a soft click, and he turned the knob to open the door. He turned to the whisperer. "We're in."

Lights came on . . . in the wine cellar, in the hallway, all over the house. Alarms sounded . . . in the wine cellar, in the hallway, all over the house. Both men jumped, frantically looking around in the blinding light as the noise blared. In the middle of the wine cellar sat an older man, pointing a handgun directly at the two men in the doorway.

Jumpy and scared, the whisperer pulled his own handgun out of his jacket pocket and fired three times at the older man, hitting him in the chest. He slumped forward in his chair, blood dripping onto the gray and white marble floor. In shock, the whisperer stood still, staring at the dead man, his handgun still in his hand.

"Perfect." Franco walked to the dead man and picked up the weapon now hanging from his limp hand. Firing once he shot the whisperer, who fell to the floor where he had been standing. He then laid the handgun back near the dead man's hand. "That worked better than I could have ever hoped."

With that, he calmly went to the control panel, shut off the alarms, and went to work. Once he had what he needed from the wine cellar, he snooped around the rest of the house and snatched a piece just for himself. This was worth the trip. Bart didn't need to know about this one.

He left just like he came. In the dark. He forgot about the paintings.

Chapter 3

Whistling and smiling to herself as she inserted her key and opened the gleaming red front door, Suzie thought about how she loved cleaning George's house. Most people refer to houses this large and stately as mansions. And, by San Francisco standards, it definitely was that. But, George was such a nice guy, and he always kept his house so inviting that Suzie thought of it as just another house she cleaned.

She was quite fond of George and his house. In fact, of all of her clients, George was her favorite. He reminded her of her grandfather, the one she lived with after her parents were killed in a boating accident. Suzie and her grandfather were inseparable during her youth. Their bond remained strong when she started college, and she helped him after hip surgery.

That's how she met George. He had developed some wonderful new component that was used in hip replacement surgeries. Her grandpa was the first patient to have the piece implanted at the Stanford Medical Center, and after that he and George became friends. She smiled and thought to herself . . . *and the rest is history. I sure wish Grandpa was still alive. He would be proud of me and my business and would love to see me get my degree. I can just see him and George drinking coffee or wine and chatting about the world. Right now, though, I need to quit reminiscing and get to work.*

Once inside, Suzie punched the alarm code into a keypad that was discretely hidden along the edge of a large painting in the spacious foyer. Continuing to talk softly to herself, she looked around, *I really do have a great business. How else would I be able to see the insides of these grand old homes in the Presidio area of San Francisco? I hope George is home today. I haven't spoken to him for a couple of weeks, and I miss our chats about his artwork. I'm learning so much.* She closed and locked the front door, looked up at the small but gleaming chandelier hanging overhead, and knew she wouldn't have to clean it today. It still sparkled from her last visit when she took it all apart and cleaned every last crystal.

"George, it's Suzie. I'll make my way to the den first, in case you're here." Turning toward the den, she stopped when she thought she heard a noise coming from that direction. "George, is that you?" Suzie continued down the hall to the left of the foyer and poked her head into the den. Nothing. "George?" No answer. No noises.

Deciding George wasn't home and that her imagination provided the noise, Suzie walked back to the closet off the kitchen that held all of her cleaning supplies. As she gathered up the things she needed to first clean the kitchen, she thought she heard another, louder noise. This one sounded like George was moving furniture upstairs.

"George, what are you doing? You aren't supposed to lift anything heavy until your shoulder heals, remember? Let me come up and help you." Placing the supplies on a kitchen counter, Suzie walked out of the kitchen and towards the staircase. The noise continued upstairs. Now more of a scraping sound, she wondered if George was sliding the furniture around in one of the large bedrooms instead of lifting it. "You can be so stubborn some times," she mumbled more to herself than out loud.

Rounding the corner at the top of the stairs, she listened to see where the noise was coming from and decided it was George's bedroom suite. "George?" No answer. Opening the door, Suzie was about to call out to George again.

That's the last thing she remembered.

Chapter 4

Her head hurt. *No*, she thought. Her head felt like it was exploding, one part at a time, and there was nothing she could do about it. She tried to blink. She tried to open her eyes. More pain and then that really bright light that kept moving around. It was annoying.

"Can you hear me? Can you open your eyes?" The voice was pleasant, almost soft. But, that damn light was beginning to get to her.

Once more she tried to focus enough to get her eyes to function. They must have fluttered a little as the nice voice came again. "Good. She's responding. Her vitals are good. And, thankfully, her head wound wasn't that serious."

It took some effort, but gradually she opened her eyes. Where was she? What happened? Why did she hurt so? Forming thoughts and trying to speak, her voice sounded weak and scratchy to her ears. "Where am I?"

"I'm Dr. Jon Thompson. You are in a hospital. You've had a head injury, and we had to make a few stitches in your head. I'm going to ask you a few questions. Okay?" She nodded. "What is your name?"

"It's Suzie Thomas."

"Good." Then Dr. Thompson asked her if she knew what day it was, if she could tell him the year, the president of the United

States, her address, and a few more simple questions. Suzie figured she must be answering them correctly, as he nodded when she answered. She held up her hand after the last question.

"Dr. Thompson, why are you asking me these? Is it because my head hurts?"

"Yes. But, it doesn't appear you've had any serious concussion, just a bump on the head requiring some stitches. You were lucky." He stepped aside, and two officers stepped forward. "I'm Officer Luke Casey, this is Officer John Street. We're with the San Francisco Police Department. Ms. Thomas, we have some questions we need to ask you. Clark Moreno here is a special investigator." Officer Casey gestured to the other man in the room. "Can you tell us what you remember before waking up here?"

Closing her eyes, Suzie tried to replay in her mind what she was doing before her head felt like an entire trainload of fireworks went off inside. When she opened her eyes, everyone was looking at her. "I'm pretty sure I remember some of what I was doing. I seem to be missing something, and it bothers me I can't get it out of my brain. Please call me Suzie."

"Okay, Suzie. Why don't you start with what you do remember? And, can you tell us if you know a man named George Hanson?"

Chapter 5

"I do know him. In fact, today was my day for cleaning George's house. He and my grandpa were friends, and I go there every week, even though he hardly needs me weekly. Today I let myself in, like I always do. George gave me a key and the alarm code when I first started cleaning his house. Sometimes he's there, and sometimes he comes back while I'm working." Suzie had been looking out the window while she spoke and now looked at the people in the room. One of the policemen and Clark were taking notes. "Oh dear, I didn't finish cleaning George's house. I didn't really get started, and I don't want him to think I just left it. I need to call him. Where is my phone?"

Clark smiled at her. "Suzie, we'll take care of that. Can you go through everything that happened once you got to Mr. Hanson's?"

Suzie nodded. "I looked in the den for George when I first got there, but he wasn't there, so I started cleaning in the kitchen. We usually sit and talk about his art, either in the den or in the kitchen. I'm learning so much from him about art and artists. Did you know he has some paintings that are worth a lot of money? He also had an art studio built in his home so he can paint." Suzie paused, took a breath, and then continued.

"I had just started cleaning in the kitchen. Oh wait . . . I had heard a noise earlier but it stopped. Since he didn't answer me when I called out, I figured George wasn't home, so I decided to start in the kitchen, but I really didn't get started. I just got out the supplies. You see, George is very particular about the scents and cleaning products I use. He buys them and keeps them there, and I use his supplies. Now I remember. I had just put the supplies on the counter, when I heard another, louder noise. It sounded like George was moving furniture in his bedroom upstairs. He's not supposed to lift anything until his doctor clears him. He had some type of surgery on his rotator cuff, I think.

"Anyway, I thought I would go help him and remind him not to lift anything. I really wasn't sure if I could help him, but I didn't want him messing up his shoulder. I headed toward the stairs, and the noise changed. It sounded more like a scratching or something scraping on the floor, like George was sliding furniture around the bedroom. I still figured I'd better try to help him. So, I called out to him as I went up the stairs, and the noise stopped.

"I remember opening the door to his bedroom. And . . ." Suzie shook her head as if trying to clear it. "And, that's it. That's all I remember. Can someone tell me what happened and why I ended up here?"

"Suzie, did you see George?"

"No. Not at all. He didn't even answer me when I called to him."

"Okay. Did you go into George's wine cellar?"

"No. Why? He doesn't have me clean in there. He has shown it to me but I leave it alone. Why? What's going on? I really should call George. He'll be worried about me."

"Suzie, we have some bad news." Clark looked somber. "George is dead."

Chapter 6

Suzie's eyes widened. "Dead? How can that be? I heard him moving around upstairs. I just saw him last week." Nothing was making sense. "Are you sure?"

"Suzie, it wasn't George you heard upstairs. It was a burglar. Officer Casey, will you please fill her in on what you found?"

"Sure. Ma'am, about 10 o'clock this morning we had a call from a neighbor who lives up the street. She said she was just coming home from walking her dog and saw a man leaving Mr. Hanson's house. He seemed to be in a hurry, had a large package in his hand, he kept his head down, and didn't wave to her when she called out to him. That's when she noticed the front door to the home was standing open. She didn't want to go in, so she called 911."

Suzie was nodding and trying to get her thoughts in order. "I arrived about nine thirty or so. And, I distinctly remember closing and locking the front door. I'll bet it was the lady who walks the Pomeranian. I don't remember her name, but she's always friendly and waves to me. What time did I come here? Are you sure George is dead?"

Officer Casey continued. "The lady's name is Lucille. When she called, we sent a patrol out to investigate and to talk to her. When they arrived at Mr. Hanson's home, the officers found the front door wide open. Upon investigation of the home, they found you and called an ambulance. You had been hit on the head and were lying on the floor. They also found Mr. Hanson. Are you sure you can handle this? You seem to know him pretty well."

Suzie nodded. "What happened?"

"Well, the two officers called for backup, and all of them carefully inspected the home. In the wine cellar they found a real mess. That's one of the reasons we called Clark."

Suzie interrupted, "Oh no. George is proud of that wine cellar, and he told me it has a lot of old wine. I hope it wasn't destroyed."

"It wasn't a mess of wine. They found Mr. Hanson, George, shot to death, and another man, also dead. Mr. Hanson was slumped in a chair in the wine cellar. He had been shot three times and had been dead for probably a day or less, according to the medical examiner. The gunshots were the cause of death, and it was probably so quick that he didn't know what hit him, again according to the ME.

On the floor was another man, one we've identified as a small-time burglar. He has a record here in San Francisco and has been arrested multiple times. He always managed to get released, using a high-priced lawyer. We also have no idea how he knew Mr. Hanson. Or, if he even knew him. Maybe he was just there to steal something. Clark has just come from the house and might have some more news.

"Clark?"

"Thanks, Officer Casey. I did just come from Mr. Hanson's home, and there are several odd, downright peculiar things about this whole crime scene. If, indeed, Mr. Hanson had been shot yesterday, why was this burglar just leaving the home today? Are the two crimes connected? What was Mr. Hanson doing in the wine cellar? Who is the burglar from today? More things just don't add up. Are you up to answering some more questions and helping us understand Mr. Hanson a little better?"

Nodding, Suzie looked at the officers and Clark. "I'll try, but I don't really know what I can tell you that you probably haven't already figured out about George." When she said his name, tears welled up in the corners of her eyes. "I just can't believe he's dead.

Do you know for sure if it was the other dead man who killed him? Is there going to be a funeral? I don't believe he had any close relatives. He used to tell me he wished he had a daughter or grand-daughter like me. Sorry. I know I'm not making much sense." Now, the tears flowed easier from Suzie's eyes, and Dr. Thompson's nurse handed her some tissues.

"Where is he? Can I see him? I think I want to."

The nurse looked at her. "Suzie, first we need to ask if you have any next of kin we need to notify."

"No. It's just me." Suzie looked down at her hands.

Placing her hand on Suzie's shoulder, the nurse motioned to Clark. "That's okay, dear. I just wanted to be sure. Clark and the officers can take you to the morgue and then back here. Dr. Thompson wants to keep you overnight, just to make certain there are no signs of a concussion. You'll most likely have a headache, and we can keep an eye on your swelling."

Clark helped the nurse as they moved Suzie into a wheelchair. "We'd like to take Suzie to the house, too, if that's okay. We'll bring her back here after we take a quick walk through of Mr. Hanson's house."

Chapter 7

The officers, Clark, and Suzie headed to the elevator and then down to the morgue, where they were all ushered into a cold anteroom. Another door opened into an even colder room, and a man with a white lab coat came forward.

"I'm Dr. Wilson. I'm sorry for your loss, Miss. If you can, I'd like for you to identify the body." He helped Suzie out of the wheelchair, took one hand, led her toward a wall of drawers, and opened one. A white sheet covered the body. "Are you sure you're ready?"

Suzie nodded and gripped Clark's hand tighter with her other hand. When Dr. Wilson pulled back the sheet to expose the face, Suzie gasped. "Yes, that's George. He looks so peaceful. I didn't know what to expect. Can we go now?"

Dr. Wilson nodded to the officers, covered the body, and shut the drawer.

On the way back upstairs, Suzie dried her tears and sniffed into her tissues. "Poor George. Who would ever want to hurt him? What did they steal from him? How did this happen?"

"Will you be okay to go to Mr. Hanson's house now? I'd like you to walk around and let us know if anything doesn't seem quite right. I've been through the house only once, after the police were there, and I found some things I'd like your help with." Clark was looking at Suzie and at the nurse who met them at the elevator. She asked Suzie how her head felt.

"My head hurts a little, but the pounding pain is gone. At least it doesn't feel like a marching band and a rock concert are trying to outdo each other anymore. I'd like to get this over with as soon as I can. By the way, what's going to happen to George's things? Does anyone know if he has any relatives? I should clean his house in case someone is coming." With that Suzie looked at the policemen.

"Right now, we don't know. We're looking into relatives. Officer Casey and I will meet you and Clark at Mr. Hanson's house." The nurse helped Suzie get dressed and wheeled her to Clark's car just outside the back entrance.

On the drive, Suzie was quiet as she thought of George.

"I have a few more questions, if it's okay with you. But, I don't want to interrupt your thoughts." Clark spoke softly to Suzie.

Nodding, Suzie said, "Sure. But I don't really think I know anything more."

"You might be surprised at what you know that would be of help to all of us. Do you know George's schedule, what he does, or who his friends are?"

"I think he has coffee or lunch with friends in North Beach. He has mentioned some names but I don't really know them and have never met them. He was taking a painting class at the university, and I know his class spent some time at the de Young Museum. I think the painting class was on Monday mornings, and they would go to the museum on Tuesday mornings. Usually, he was home all day Friday when I cleaned. He would talk to me about what they did in class that week."

"Did he ever show you his paintings?"

"Oh yes. I liked the colors but couldn't quite grasp what he was trying to do. Every one of them always looked like a bunch of squiggly, white lines in really bright swatches of color. In fact, when he asked me what I saw in them, I told him the colors made me think of a giant sky at sunset, and the lines looked like prehistoric birds. I remember asking him if the next one was going to be different. He laughed at me." Suzie wiped the tears slipping out of her eyes. "I so enjoyed talking to him."

"Do you know where he kept his paintings?"

"Sure. Some were hanging downstairs; there were a couple in the wine cellar, I think, and each bedroom upstairs had one. Why? Are they missing? If the thief stole those, I'm sure they're not that valuable. He has two or three small ones that are worth much more in the den and the living room. He was trying to educate me on Monet, Manet, Picasso, and someone else. I thought he said he had two paintings or sketches worth over a hundred thousand dollars. I can't imagine spending that much on a painting." Suzie shook her head and looked at Clark.

"You're sure he had paintings hanging in the wine cellar?"

"Positive. There used to be only one. But, about a month ago he finished his latest one and showed me where he had it hung. They were on opposite walls. One was bluer, and the other one had lots of orange in it. Are they gone?"

"We'll check. For now, let's talk more about people George knew. Did he have anyone working for him; anyone that came to his house regularly?"

"Well, he had this one guy come in and help him hang his paintings, unload boxes of new painting supplies, and probably any other heavy work George couldn't do, especially after his surgery. I don't really know how often he came."

"Did you ever meet him or know his name?"

"I met him one time. He wasn't that friendly, and I really wondered why George would have him come back. He hardly spoke at all, and when he did, it was a mumble. I think his name was Franco, but I don't know his last name."

"That's good. It gives us something to go on."

Chapter 8

Clark continued. "When I looked around, I found George's laptop, which some police technicians are inspecting, and his calendar with several appointments on it. I saw his painting classes listed, some lunch dates, doctor appointments, and then one day completely blocked out with a name on it. I want to know if you have ever heard George mention the name Marta Swenson."

"I'm not sure. Why? Who is she?"

"Well, she's a dear friend of mine and a travel consultant who lives here in San Francisco part time, in Venice part time, and . . ."

Suzie interrupted. "Wait. George was all excited about going to Venice to visit a friend as soon as his doctor told him it was okay to go. He had a fancy, old bracelet he wanted the friend to take to someone who lives there. I think he said he sent a photo of it to her. One time he showed it to me, and it was quite spectacular. I had never seen anything like it. Could she be the friend?"

"She could be. The thing is . . . she's supposed to meet with George this coming week. That's too much of a coincidence for me, that's all."

Smiling, Suzie stared out the window as she remembered all the things she loved about George and his home. Thinking to herself that it wouldn't be the same without George there, she wanted to see his home one last time. But, when they drove into the driveway it didn't look like the last time she entered. Yellow police tape was strung around the entire house, yard, and shrubbery.

"Oh, dear. It looks terrible. George wouldn't have liked this look. He was so particular about how his home looked. When will this all be removed?"

"It has to stay this way for now, at least until the police gather all the information they can from here. At the moment, it's still a crime scene. I know it looks terrible, but it's for the best, Suzie.

"If you're ready, let's go inside. I want you to look at everything closely. Let me know if something is out of place or missing. No detail is insignificant, and nothing is too small to be mentioned. Ready?"

Taking a deep breath, Suzie nodded. "Let's look."

Chapter 9

Suzie led the way, followed by Clark and Officers Casey and Street. Nodding more to herself than anyone else, she noticed nothing out of place until they entered the den. "See that spot above the fireplace? One of George's paintings was hanging there. Now, it's gone. And, the small painting he did that used to hang over here is missing, too." She gestured to the right of the doorway. "But, the one he said was worth the most money is still here." Suzie pointed to the bookshelf. "See. It's still on the easel George had made for it."

"Are you sure the missing ones were both there recently? Could he have moved either of them?"

"I don't think he would move them. He really liked to sit here, read, and look at his paintings. Or, at least that's what he told me."

"Okay. We'll make a note of that and keep going."

When they entered the wine cellar, Suzie's eyes immediately went to the red stain on the otherwise pristine marble floor. A small gasp escaped as she looked away. Officer Casey steadied her. "Are you okay? I'm sorry you have to see this, Suzie. We cleaned up what we could, but the floor needs to be professionally cleaned. Do you want to leave?"

"No. I'm okay. It just seems so real when I actually see it." Suzie closed her eyes. When she reopened them, she looked around the room, avoiding the floor. "George had two paintings in here. One used to be on this wall, and it's gone. This one, however, is still here. I wonder why the thief only took one of them. They looked almost the same."

"Hmmm. I see what you mean about the colors and the squiggly lines, Suzie." Clark was looking closely at the small painting. "Officers, I'd like to take this for closer inspection. I'll clear it with your superiors and anyone else I need to. I have some art paper in my car to wrap it in."

Officer Casey nodded, "They said you could take any of the paintings. We'll just have you sign later. You might as well take them now, as long as we're here."

Looking puzzled, Suzie asked Clark, "What are you going to inspect them for?"

"Let me fill you in a little more about me, Suzie. I'm a retired Marine, now an FBI special investigator dealing with stolen art and wines, and I consult with Interpol at times. I just finished working with an art heist in Dubai and am due in Italy next week to consult on some possible forgeries. That's why the art here has me interested. If I can look at this better in my lab, I might find some clues, considering the thief stole some of George's work and left the small Monet in his den. Although, that one may be a copy and not an original, based on its size. I'll inspect it as well. We may be dealing with a smart thief or a very dumb one."

Suzie nodded at Clark's explanation. "You mean George's own paintings might be valuable?"

"Maybe. More likely, though, they may hold another clue for something. I'm just not sure what, at this point. Do you know if he ever had any other businesses or worked with any art dealers?"

"Not really. He mentioned names of friends or guys he went to lunch with . . . but no art dealers. As for business dealings, I do know he made a great deal of money from the hip replacement device he invented. And, he was always drawing and sketching. His sketch journal was with him all the time. I think he was a mechanical engineer at one time, and his drawings reminded me of machines. He loved those drawings. I remember him saying he needed to show different drawings to somebody, but I don't know who. They didn't mean anything to me. Did you find his journal?"

"I don't believe so. We'll talk to some of his friends later. Do you see anything else out of place here in the cellar?"

"I was only in here a few times with George. He never had me clean in here, so I don't know if any wine is missing or how much he had here." Suzie was still avoiding looking at the red stained floor.

"That's fine." Clark had been surveying the racks of wine as Suzie was talking and now squatted down to look at the lower shelf along the left side. "Hmm. Something's not quite right." He stepped back to look at the racks above and then the ones on the right side. "It appears George had a system here, and things are out of place in this area, judging by the bottle sizes and ages."

"Oh yes. That's one reason he said I didn't need to clean in here. He had his system and didn't want it to be messed with. He has a whole list of his wines, and he knows exactly where they are. In the last month he was just starting to teach me about wines. I like drinking different wine but didn't know much about any of them. George loved to teach, and he was going to teach me about different grapes."

"Do you know where he kept his list?"

"I think he had a printed list somewhere in this drawer." Suzie opened the small drawer in the tasting counter, moved a couple of corkscrews and a polishing cloth, and found what she was looking for. "I think this is it. I'm not sure how often he printed it, though. It may not be useful if it's not current."

Clark unfolded the list, looked at the wines on the shelves, compared them to the list, and again knelt down to the lower left side. "That's what was wrong. These are in the wrong place. Some wines are missing."

Chapter 10

Putting on his gloves, Clark carefully removed six bottles from the bottom left shelf and six from a shelf above it. Setting them on the tasting counter, he checked the printed list, and went to a shelf about halfway up along the opposite side. That space was empty, except for two other bottles.

"Look. These 12 bottles belong with the two in this part of the cellar. George apparently kept his oldest wines along the left side, right down here. It appears his most valuable ones were stored on these bottom shelves. But, the 12 I just pulled from there are not terribly valuable. Sure, they're great wines . . . just not valuable by George's standard or according to his chart.

"Which means there are bottles missing, if I'm reading his chart correctly. That could be what the thief was after. I'm just not sure why."

"But, wouldn't the thief have to know they were here?" Suzie had been looking around the wine cellar and now at Clark. "Would you kill for wine? Was it really worth that much?"

"Suzie, the wine that appears to be missing is great wine, but not really worth killing over. There has to be more going on here. Other things are bothering me about this wine cellar as well. First, what the hell was George doing in his wine cellar late at night? Was he just sitting here? There's got to be more to it than we're seeing.

Next, you are correct in asking if the thief knew what wine was here. Do you know if George talked about his wine a lot? Maybe he mentioned it to his lunch buddies. Also, how would the thief know the code to open the door, assuming it was locked? And, once more, maybe most important . . . what the hell was George doing sitting in his wine cellar?"

The two police officers and Suzie looked at Clark. Officer Street spoke first. "The ME said he died here. He wasn't killed somewhere else and moved here. But why here? You're right, Clark. I mean, you don't usually just sit in your wine cellar and wait for someone to come in, do you?"

"Not at all. Which makes me wonder if he was expecting them. But, why? Let's finish going through the house. I'm going to have to think about the wine puzzle. Officers, can you make a copy of this for me? There's something I'm not catching right now." Clark handed the list of wines to Officer Street.

Both officers nodded to Clark. The rest of the downstairs was in order as far as Suzie could tell. "There's nothing missing that I'm aware of. It looks like it does when I clean."

Upstairs, the first three bedrooms and bathrooms looked the same to Suzie as well. "I'm just not seeing anything missing or out of the ordinary. His paintings are still hanging in all the regular places. Sorry, Clark." She started to open the door to George's bedroom, the one where she was hit on the head, and hesitated.

"Suzie, are you sure you can handle this? Let me go in first." Clark stepped in front of her, and took her hand.

Slowly Suzie entered . . . and gasped.

"Things are missing. George's favorite things are missing." She sat down on the nearest chair and looked at Clark. "But, this is the other painting he told me was valuable. It's still here." Suzie pointed to the wall above George's nightstand.

"What's missing, Suzie? What should we be looking for?"

Chapter 11

"Well, the first thing I noticed is a painting is missing. George was so proud of the painting that hung above his desk. It was his best, according to him."

"What was the painting?"

"More colorful swishes and more prehistoric birds, I guess. It really didn't look a whole lot different than the others. Just larger and perhaps bolder." Suzie shrugged. "But, he really liked it. He said it was his final key. I have no idea what he meant."

"And yet, this one is still here." Clark stepped closer to the one above the nightstand. "It appears to be another Monet, although I'm skeptical. What else do you see?"

"Well, this door is open." Suzie pointed to a door at the back of the bedroom. "It's George's painting studio, and he always keeps it closed. Always. He has a special ventilation system, so he doesn't get paint smells anywhere else in the house. This door is never left open." Suzie walked toward the studio, looked in, and jumped back. "Oh no. This is terrible."

The studio was a mess. Tubes of paint littered the floor, some broken, canvases were ripped apart, and an easel lay on its side. "Somebody was looking for something in here." Clark turned to the officers. "It was like this when I was here as well. Do you know if it was noted in the preliminary investigation?"

"Yes. The room was dusted for prints, but we only found ones belonging to Mr. Hanson. We left it like this because we weren't sure if there was something missing."

"Suzie, can you tell at a glance if something is missing? Do you come in here to clean?"

"I don't clean in here. I've been in here a few times when George showed me his work in progress, but that's all. I really wouldn't know if anything is missing." After looking at the mess in the studio, they all came back into the bedroom. Suzie looked around and walked to his desk. "But, there is something missing here. George had a small chest sitting right here on his desk, and it's gone."

"Maybe he moved it." Clark looked around the room. "How big is it? Can you describe it? Do you know what is in it?"

"Better than that. I have a picture on my phone. Where's my purse? Is it still downstairs, or did it get taken to the hospital?"

Officer Casey nodded. "We found a small, red purse in the entry way and took it to the hospital with you. It's probably still locked up with your other things. We can get it when we take you back."

"Good. I'll try to describe it, and then you can see the picture I have. The chest sat right here, so you can see it's not very large. It reminded me of an old pirate chest with a gold cross on the top. There was a lock hanging on the front, but it wasn't a real lock. It just looked like one. George only opened it one time to show me what was in it. He said it was the only thing he had from his mother's family. It was the most beautiful bracelet I had ever seen. This is the piece he talked about when he mentioned going to Venice. He was so proud of that bracelet and hoped he could learn more about it. Does the lady you mentioned know about old chests and jewelry?"

"I do know Marta has some fantastic pieces her grandmother left to her, and she works with a jeweler in Venice. Last year she discovered fascinating history about her grandmother's family based on that jewelry. Perhaps George wanted to visit with her about all of that." Clark motioned toward the bedroom door. "I think we're finished for now. We need to get you back to the hospital, Suzie. I need to check in with Marta, and we should all get together tomorrow. I think Dr. Thompson will release you by then, if you're doing okay."

Chapter 12

Suzie was back in the hospital, and Clark was on his way to see Marta when his phone rang. It was Special Agent Ian Wells from Interpol, Clark's main contact person when working on anything art related.

"Clark, more paintings surfaced in Italy. One collector in Milan just had his painting re-authenticated as he kept having dreams about it. Turns out his dreams were nightmares. His three million dollar Picasso is worth about one hundred dollars. It looks good . . . but it's not real. As you can imagine, he's upset. The other one is a Monet forgery that came to an auction house in Rome. They investigate before putting anything in their catalogue, and this one is definitely a fake. Supposedly, the lady who owned it died, and her nephew had placed everything with the auction house. He had no idea it was fake, or so he says. Italian police and our guys are questioning him as we speak. I'm wrapping up a case here in London and will be heading there next. How soon can you get to Venice?"

"Give me a few days. I'm working on a case here in San Francisco with the SFPD involving a murder, art theft, and I'm not sure what else. You remember Marta? It appears she may be connected to the victim, and I'm on my way to see her. She just came back from Venice today. By the way, does a thief by the name of Franco, no known last name yet, mean anything to you?"

"Not off the top of my head, but I'll do some checking. San Francisco based?"

"Yeah, I think so. He may have stolen about 12 bottles of semi-valuable wine, some not so valuable artwork, and an old chest with a flashy bracelet in it. Turns out he left the most valuable pieces of art in the house, and we aren't sure why. It's confusing right now. I'll be in touch later. Right now I'm going to check in with Marta and then head to my lab to look at a couple of paintings the thief left behind."

"Okay. I'll check with agencies on a thief named Franco and get back to you."

∾

Clark arrived at Marta's home. Marta greeted him with a kiss as Shadow greeted him with a loud meow. "My two favorite people in the world." Clark kissed Marta and bent down to rub Shadow's back.

"Clark, I can't wait to tell you what I found. I'm so afraid of getting my hopes up. But, something tells me I found more of Grandma's history. By the way, you do realize he's a cat and not a person, don't you?" Marta pointed to Shadow as she closed the door behind Clark.

"Yeah, but don't tell him that. He might take offense." Clark had brought two paintings from George's house into the foyer and now took them to the living room.

"What do you have there?"

"First, tell me what you found that you're so excited about. You can hardly stand still, so it must be great news. Then, I'll fill you in on an art theft and murder case I just became involved in with the SFPD. You may know the victim; George Hanson."

"No! It can't be. Oh my God, I do know him. Dead? I'm supposed to meet with him. What happened?" Marta picked up Shadow and sat down. Shaking her head, she rubbed Shadow's head. "No. No. Oh my. I can't believe it. Yeah. He was just here at a party a couple of months ago, and we discovered our grand-mothers had both left us some fantastic jewelry pieces. When I filled him in on how I learned my grandmother came from a royal family, he was all excited. He told me his grandmother had left him a bracelet and another piece of jewelry, but he didn't know any-thing about them. I figured they were nice pieces, and I offered to take a photo to Sam, my jeweler and appraiser friend in Venice. I sort of forgot about all of it. Then, about two weeks ago when I was still in Venice, he emailed me photos of the bracelet." Marta stood and started pacing around the room.

"Clark, you're not going to believe this. From his photos, his grandmother's bracelet looked like it could have been a match to my grandma's necklace and tiara. If they are somehow connected, George and I may be related. I didn't tell him any of this. I really wanted to see the bracelet in person before I mentioned anything.

He was going to come to Venice with it, and we were going to take it to Sam, but George had to delay the trip due to some unplanned surgery. So, I made arrangements to come here, meet with him, and look at the bracelet. That way I could describe it to Sam. I was excited to see it for myself.

"Then, this is the most amazing thing. Three days ago I was going through another of Grandma's diaries and found one devoted entirely to what she knew about her royal family's jewels. She even has the jeweler's name, the one the family commissioned to make all these pieces. I was just beginning to read some of the history of the tiara. But, that's not all. I had just picked up the diary and guess what. Five old, black and white photos were folded and stuffed in the back. They're in bad shape, but I can definitely see the tiara and my necklace.

"There's more. There might be two necklaces, according to the photos. But, and this is why I'm meeting with George . . . or, why I was going to meet with George. There are two photos of bracelets. Bracelets. Can you believe it? The best part is, they all match. All of them! And, George's photo looks just like the old photos from Grandma.

"George could be my uncle or cousin or something. Anyway, he was going to show me the bracelet when we met this week, and then he was coming to Venice. I can't believe he's dead." Marta had been walking around the room, gesturing to Clark. She stopped, took a breath, and shook her head. "Sorry about talking so fast, but it's just so exciting. But, he's dead. Wow."

"Marta, I am so sorry about George. And, I am so fascinated by what you found." Clark hugged Marta as she stood in the center of the living room.

"Sorry to be crass. But, do you have the bracelet? Sorry. I shouldn't ask. You have bigger things to think about."

"Sadly, Marta, we do not. The chest he had it in is missing from his home, along with several paintings. These are a couple of his paintings." Clark was unwrapping the two in Marta's living room.

"As in paintings George paints or artwork he collects?"

"What he paints. Maybe you can tell me if you see anything in it." Clark filled Marta in on everything as Shadow watched from his perch at the window, purring when one of them stopped to pet him. "I want your first impressions, and then take a second look. I haven't had time to inspect them closely, yet." He turned them around so the sun highlighted the colors.

"Whoa. He must have liked blue and orange, huh? Were these hanging together or are they supposed to go together?" Marta turned them first toward the light and then away from it, so shadows appeared over them. Then, she turned them again. "Hmm." She rearranged them and turned them upside down. "Aha. Did you see this?"

Clark had been watching her and the paintings as she moved them. Marta was learning about art investigation from him and from a mentor in Venice, and she was learning quickly. Now, he moved closer to her. "Tell me what is so interesting."

"Well, upon first glance I think of them as nicely done abstract scenes. They could be sunsets, sunrises, or just color combinations he loved. He may have even been practicing some technique. The blending is well done, no obvious brush lines, and pretty. Very pretty. The white figures scattered throughout could be clouds, waves, birds, or nothing in particular. Are there more like these two?"

"I'm not sure. But, you saw something else, didn't you?"

"I don't know. Watch this. When I turn this one upside down, the white figures become numbers. Or, at least with some imagination, they do. Look."

"Well, I'll be. Definitely. Does the other one do the same thing?"

"Kind of, but they're harder to decipher. This one has what looks like three numbers and two lines that are just lines. Do you really suppose they're numbers or is this just a quirky coincidence?"

"I'm not sure. I need to get all of his paintings and then talk to his art instructors. I'll call Officer Casey. Can you call the art department while I go pick up the rest of the paintings?"

"Sure. Come back here when you're finished; we can have dinner, and compare notes."

Chapter 13

Franco slammed his cell phone on the quasi-wood desk after he hung up from talking to Bart. "Who the hell does he think he's dealing with, anyway?" He paced around the small motel room, kicking the only chair out of the way, and tossing the remote control at the pillows on the bed. "I'm not an imbecile. He didn't tell me he wanted paintings that look like amateur drawings. I thought he was talking about real paintings, not stupid little nothings. He's supposed to be the genius when it comes to paintings. Plus, I've already been there twice. He keeps changing the rules. Now I have to go back there again. Damn!"

He glanced at his watch, and mumbled to himself. "It's too early to go back to the house now. Probably still crawling with cops." Deciding he'd get something to eat, drive by the house for a quick check, and then come back here and make plans, Franco looked at his plane ticket. He had three days before he left for Venice. "I need to pack the fancy little chest with the bracelet real good. Don't want no airline guy stealing it from me. That's my ticket to richville. Then I can pack the wine and the paintings in the cartons Bart sent." He glanced at the stash sitting in the corner.

"Guess I'll just leave the pretty paintings here when I head to Venice. Bart says they're worthless, and I don't want to take them with me. The maid can just have a present. I still don't know why the ones he wants are better. But, then again, he's paying me for those. No sense hanging on to these."

When his cell phone chirped again, Franco glanced at the screen. "I just hung up. What's he want now? Probably thought of a few more names he can call me. Tough. I'm not answering it." When it stopped ringing, Franco turned it to vibrate. "He can call me later. Right now, I'm hungry and thirsty. I need a beer."

He stuck the silent cell phone in his pocket and made his way to the parking lot, never seeing the gray sedan across the street. Behind the darkened windows sat a lone figure holding a camera with a long lens, taking photos as Franco got in his car and left the lot.

Nodding to himself, the man put down the camera and silently made his way to Franco's room. "That's him. Now I can check his room, find the jewelry Bart wants, and relieve him of it. He's in for a surprise when he gets back."

Chapter 14

"I found a total of four paintings, and Suzie is pretty sure there were at least seven, probably more. When I stopped by the hospital to talk to her, Dr. Thompson told me he is releasing her later today. Did you manage to talk to any of his instructors?" Clark was back at Marta's house, and they were having a glass of wine on the patio.

"I called the university and inquired about George and his classes. It was just dumb luck that I was able to talk to the only instructor there. I said George was my uncle, and I wanted to know how his art classes were progressing. I didn't mention he was dead or that there was a murder investigation.

"After the instructor finished chuckling, he filled me in on the so-called classes. Apparently, there's a group of five men all about George's age who take classes one day a week. It sounds like they do more talking, eating doughnuts, and drinking coffee than painting. The instructor wasn't even sure if any of them had completed any work. Currently, they're all working on landscapes, trying out different colors. Then, it sounds like they all go to lunch, and the next week, start all over again. Once in a while they go to the de Young Museum. I didn't get the impression this was serious art or even real painting lessons. It's more of an excuse to get together. He didn't think any of them ever took any canvases, complete or not, home. So, my guess is George's paintings weren't done there."

Marta shrugged her shoulders. "Did you have a chance to look at the rest from his house?"

"I brought them all here. But, if what the instructor said was true about George not taking any canvases home, then you're right, and he wasn't working on these at a class. This was something he was doing only in his home studio. I wonder why? Let's unwrap them and look at them in the light in the living room." Clark led the way to where the paintings sat in Marta's living room. Shadow was sniffing the wrapping and meowed as Clark scratched his back.

Once they were lined up along the wall, Marta gestured to them. "I don't know about you, but to me they all look about the same. Different sizes. Blues, oranges, and pinks in all the backgrounds. White lines in every one. That's kind of weird, don't you think? Maybe he just liked these colors and was trying to perfect a certain style, whatever that style might be."

"Let's assume we're seeing numbers in those white lines. Are they a bank account number, an offshore account, or a combination? And, if Suzie is correct, and there are supposed to be more of them, so what? Or, are we grasping at nothing; they're really just seagulls, and George liked to paint them? Marta, let's switch gears a minute. What do you know about George?"

"I really didn't know him that well. I was so hoping the bracelet would lead us to more information about his grandma, my grandma, and our possible mutual family history. Damn. I really hoped we were related. It would be nice to have an uncle. But, our mutual friend who invited him to my party might have some better information. I think you know him. It's Peter, who owns Peter's Italian Café. We could go there tomorrow morning for coffee."

Chapter 15

Franco returned to the motel, hanging on to his six-pack of beer in a brown paper bag in one hand and his room key and the bag with the chest in it in the other hand. Once he managed to get the door unlocked and partially open, he dropped the beer and grabbed his handgun from the middle of his back. The lights were on, and his things were strewn about the room. Carefully he opened the door farther, his eyes taking in the mess.

Checking the bathroom and under the bed, Franco decided no one was still there. Picking up the beer, he peeked through the curtains to the back parking lot. Shadows in the dusk didn't provide any clues. "How could I have been so stupid? Who's watching me? I need to get out of here."

Packing up his clothes and few belongings didn't take long. "I'm glad I had this sweet piece of jewelry with me. I bet that's what they were looking for. I'm going to find another place to crash and leave the paintings here. Bart said they weren't worth anything anyway," he mumbled.

Walking in the shadows, around the building, and crouching between a van and a truck, Franco carefully made his way to the parking lot where he left his car. When he left the parking lot, he drove side streets and alleys, always checking the rearview mirror. He even stopped by a police car and pretended to make a phone call. Satisfied no one had followed him, he checked into another old motel a couple of miles away from the first one.

Barricading the door, he double-checked the window, and saw nothing. Satisfied he was still alone, he lay down on the bed fully clothed with his handgun under the pillow. "I'll have to stay out of sight for another day, and then I can break into George's mansion and grab the last two things Bart wants. I can't wait to get out of town."

His phone rang, making him jump about a foot in the air. Looking at the screen, he swore. "Damn. I'd better answer it.

"Hello, Bart. Yeah, I had my phone on vibrate and didn't hear it. I was having dinner and thought I'd call you back. What's up?" He listened while Bart barked out new instructions. Nodding his head, he tried to speak when Bart paused.

"You're kidding. She's alive? I hit her pretty hard. I'll bet that old lady with the yappy dog called the police, or she would have laid there for a long time. They were at his mansion? Yeah, sure, I told you I can do it. No, I got it. I'll give it another day, and things will have calmed down. There'll be another murder, and the cops will have moved on. No big deal. Yeah, right.

"I already told you, I'll get those other two paintings. I know exactly where they are. Easy for me. No, I don't know where the cleaning woman lives. Is she still in the hospital? What? She knows me? How? Yeah, I have a pen. Calm down. I'll take care of it. Give me her address. Okay, got it. No, I'll take care of her. I'll see . . ." Franco heard silence in the phone as Bart hung up.

"What a jerk. He thinks I can't finish a job. He thinks I don't know what to do. I'll show him. He doesn't mess with Franco." Upset, Franco opened a beer and gulped down half of it in one swig. "Wait a minute. Bart sure knows a lot about what's going on here. How? I thought he was in Venice. How does he know what's going on in San Francisco? I need to be careful."

$\mathcal{C}$hapter 16

"Sorry about that, Marta and Clark. It got busy about the time you guys got here. Someone told me you wanted to talk to me. What's up?" Peter wiped his hands on his apron and took a long drink of his coffee.

"Peter, thanks for taking a few minutes this morning. Clark and I would like to talk to you about George Hanson. I believe you're the one who introduced him to me." Marta smiled sadly. "Have you heard about what happened?"

"No. Did something happen to George? He and his pals come in here at least once a month for coffee, but I haven't seen him for a few weeks. Is he okay?"

Clark looked at Peter. "I'm sorry to have to tell you this, but George was killed at his home two days ago. Marta and I are trying to track down any relatives of George's and also talk to his friends. But, we aren't sure where to start. Anything you can tell us would be greatly appreciated."

"Oh dear. That's terrible. I assume the police are involved. Any idea what happened?"

Marta nodded her head. "Yes, the police are involved. His cleaning lady walked in on a robbery and was hurt. When the police investigated, they found George dead in his wine cellar. They found another man, presumably the killer, also dead.

George and I were going to meet this week about some things his grandmother left to him. It appears we might have some history in common. But, the piece he wanted to show me is missing. So, like Clark said, we are trying to find relatives and close friends. All we have to go on is his calendar in his home and whatever the cleaning lady knows. No address book, no contacts on his computer, and not much else. Did he ever talk about family or mention relatives?"

Peter was shaking his head. "Poor George. He was such a great guy. Loved life. In fact, I thought he had plans to go to Italy fairly soon."

"Yes. He was going to come visit me once we talked about his grandmother's jewelry. In fact, I was excited to have him meet my friend in Venice who specializes in that type of jewelry. But, you never heard him mention a son or a daughter or grandkids?"

"No. Maybe his buddies know. I know most of them and could call them. They might have a better idea. Let me get my phone, and I'll make the calls. Do they know he's dead? What should I tell them?"

Clark looked at Peter. "If you call them and tell them I'm a friend of George, I can handle the rest of the conversation. Would that work?"

Peter nodded, made the calls, and introduced Clark who visited with five different men about George. All were saddened and shocked to hear about him. Hanging up from talking with the last one, Clark looked at Marta and Peter.

"The good news is they won't have to read about George in the paper. But, not a one ever heard him mention any relatives, close or distant. One guy, Charlie, has known George for a long time, too. Apparently he knew about George's company and his inventions. It seems George had a partner at one time and they had a serious falling out. I mean serious. George told Charlie the partner was slime and a no-good scoundrel. George's words, according to him. Apparently, George had spent a bunch of time and money making sure the ex-partner stayed out of the picture. He talked about it a few times to one of the other guys, who is a retired federal judge. Charlie thought the ex-partner either died or moved away, until recently when George mentioned a problem he needed to deal with. It concerned the ex-partner, apparently. Then, Charlie asked if I knew about George's inventions. I told him Suzie, the cleaning lady, talked about some medical device George invented. But, Charlie said George had all sorts of patents and inventions, not just one. George told Charlie and the rest of the guys he kept everything safe so the no-good ex-partner wouldn't find anything. George was clever, according to Charlie. And, Charlie seems to think all his inventions and plans are worth serious money, but that was speculation on his part.

"But, again, no mention of family. Charlie and the rest of the guys would show grandkid pictures, but not George. If anyone noticed he didn't have any, they never mentioned it. So far, it's a dead-end on relatives."

Peter had been nodding as Clark related what he learned. "If I talk to anyone else about George, I'll let you know. But, those are the guys who should know him best. Sorry about that."

"Thanks, Peter."

Chapter 17

Suzie cleared it with her physician and the officers who were finished processing George's home. She explained to them she needed to clean George's home one last time. She had no idea if relatives were coming or not, but she knew she needed closure. It was important to her. Suzie gathered up her cleaning cloths and muttered to herself as she headed out the door of her condo. "This will be a sad job today. Especially in the wine cellar."

She had just turned onto the walkway into the parking lot when she almost ran into a man delivering flowers. "Excuse me. I guess I need to watch where I'm going. Oh, somebody's getting some pretty flowers." The guy kept walking. "That's odd. Most deliverymen in this area are friendly. Wonder what's wrong with him."

Part way to George's house, Suzie had a thought. *That delivery guy reminds me of someone. But, I don't know who. And, it's not like I know anyone that surly or unhappy. He has such an enjoyable job, too.*

Pulling up to George's home, Suzie parked in the driveway and noticed the yellow police tape was gone. "That's good. I was going to take it down if it was still here. I hope my key still works. I'll have to give it to the police when I'm done today. It will be so sad to leave this beautiful home. But, it's sadder that George is no longer here." She didn't notice the white car following her. She didn't see the driver park down the street from George's driveway.

Once inside, Suzie closed the front door, and out of habit called out to George before she caught herself. Tears welled up in her eyes. "Poor George. I really hope he didn't suffer. I wish there was something I could have done."

Thinking she would clean the wine cellar last, Suzie headed upstairs and started putting everything away in George's studio. "I wonder what's going to happen to all of this." She put all the opened tubes of paint in a box, threw away broken brushes, and stacked the new canvases. Picking up ones that were destroyed, she noticed something sticking out of the back of one ripped canvas. At first glance, it appeared to be part of the canvas backing, but looking further she discovered it was George's journal. He had shown the substantial black journal to her a couple of times, and now she sat down to look through it. When she saw his notes about their talks, tears spilled out, and she wiped her nose. Flipping through the rest, several entries caught her eye.

"Wow. These drawings look impressive. George has them numbered and lots of notes about some of them. I bet these are related to George's inventions he talked about. But, it's odd he put the journal in here. It's almost as if he didn't want this to be seen, and he hid it here on purpose. I need to take this to the police. I'll drop it off when I return the key." She stuck the journal in her top, left apron pocket along with her cleaning rags.

Satisfied she was finished in his studio, she shut the door and turned around to survey the bedroom.

She screamed. One shot rang out, and Suzie fell to the floor.

Chapter 18

"I've called Suzie and left a message. Marta, let's stop by the police station to fill the officers in on what Peter and Charlie told us about George's inventions and his ex-partner. I'm not sure how it fits, but it is a piece of the puzzle we didn't have before. And, I'll try Suzie again to see if she and George talked about any inventions along with his drawings." Clark and Marta headed toward the parking ramp.

"Clark, let's drive by George's house on the way to the police station. Maybe one of the officers is there, wrapping up everything."

"Great idea. I think Officer Casey said Suzie wanted to clean his house in case relatives were coming, so maybe she is there as well. Listening to Peter and then to George's friends, it certainly doesn't appear like there are any relatives. I guess he probably has a will, and that might mention someone. Maybe the officers will have found something by now."

As Clark and Marta pulled up to George's house, Lucille and her Pomeranian were standing across the street. Lucille picked up the little dog and hurried to their car. "I know something's wrong. Clyde and I just returned home from the groomer, and we were going for a walk. Something happened in George's house again. I just know things like this. I was just going to call the police and have them come check. Are you here to visit George? He's dead, you know. Who are you?" Lucille was rambling as she started walking toward the front door, the Pomeranian in her arms.

Marta couldn't help but notice that the fluffy, happy, little dog and Lucille were a fitting pair. Lucille bounced on her toes almost as much as the Pom did when he walked. They even smiled alike.

"I'm Clark, a private investigator, and this is Marta, a friend of George's." Clark reached out to pet the dog and intercepted Lucille before she could get to the front door. The Pom licked his hand, and Lucille stopped.

"Oh you poor dear." She looked at Marta. "I'm sorry for you that George died. He was such a nice man. How did you know him?"

"Lucille, we've just come from visiting with some other friends of George's, and we wondered if you know if he has any relatives we need to notify. Is there anyone you can think of?" Clark and Marta had positioned themselves in front of the door as Clark was talking, and Marta pointed to the car in the driveway. "Isn't that Suzie's car, Clark? She must be here cleaning or tidying up."

Lucille wiped a tear from her eye and motioned to the front door. "Clyde and I just got home. We should go in and talk to her. I feel so sorry for her, too. She was good for George."

Clark walked to the car and felt the hood. "It's still warm, so she's probably here somewhere. I'll check." He moved to the front door and rang the doorbell. No answer. Since the door was slightly ajar, he pushed it open with his foot and called in. "Suzie, it's Clark, Marta, and Lucille. Are you cleaning?" Hearing nothing, he pulled his weapon from a shoulder holster and whispered to Marta. "Something's not right. Call Officer Casey and stay here with Lucille."

"Oh dear, Clyde. That man has a gun. What's he going to do?" Lucille grabbed the poor Pomeranian tighter.

Marta was talking to Officer Casey when Clark yelled from inside.

"Marta, call an ambulance. Suzie's been shot. Tell them to step on it."

Chapter 19

Feeling pleased with the day's events so far, Franco picked up some food and headed to the motel. "I've finally got everything Bart wants, and that woman can't identify me anymore. I'll be on my way outta here tomorrow. Then I can disappear and live without having to think about money or people."

The two small paintings he had just grabbed from George's home were on the front seat of his car, wedged in behind the brown sack that held his six-pack of beer. The box with the wine sat in the back seat and the pizza box lay on the floor, aromas of warm pepperoni and cheese wafting up from inside the box. Franco pulled into the motel parking lot, reached under the passenger side seat, and pulled out the small chest with the shiny bracelet in it. Smiling, he mumbled to himself. "Sure glad I hid this in here and didn't leave it in my room. No telling what the maid would do if she saw it. Probably steal it."

He turned off the car, took the key from the ignition, and had just turned to open the driver side door when a bullet entered the backside of his head.

He never saw it coming and never felt a thing.

The shooter opened the passenger side door, picked up the two paintings, shut the door, took the box of wine from the back, and placed a call.

"It's Stewart. Yeah, I've got the stuff. The thief is dead. See you in a few days." He looked back and noticed the chest in the now dead man's lap. Opening the door once again, he reached over and picked up the chest, opened it, and smiled. "What do we have here? Nice. I think I just got a bonus."

With that, he pocketed the bracelet, tossed the chest back in the front seat, and quietly left the scene.

Chapter 20

Sirens from police cars and an ambulance had poor Clyde, the Pomeranian, shaking in Lucille's arms. Clark had come running out of the house right after Marta called in the 911, and now things were happening quickly and noisily. Marta ushered Lucille and Clyde over to the other side of the street, out of the way.

"What's going on? Who's dead? I hope it's not that poor girl, the one who cleans George's house. She's always so friendly. Oh dear." Lucille clutched the Pomeranian tighter as she looked at Marta.

"Lucille, let's see what Clark has to say. He must think Suzie is still alive or he wouldn't have had me call an ambulance. May I hold Clyde?" Lucille nodded and handed the little dog to Marta as they sat next to each other on the steps. Clyde seemed relieved to be released from Lucille's strong hug and settled on Marta's lap.

It seemed like a long time, but after only a few minutes Clark made his way across the street as the ambulance pulled out, sirens blaring. Marta covered Clyde's ears as he licked her hand. Two more police cars pulled up and Officers Casey and Street made their way over to the group. "Clark, what's going on? Are our guys in the house?"

"Yeah. There are four guys checking out the place. I found Suzie when I went upstairs. She looks pretty bad." Clark had turned away from Lucille and ushered the officers back across the street. "From the shell casing on the floor, it appears to be a single gunshot. Lots of blood. Not sure exactly where she was shot, but it didn't look like her head. She couldn't have been there long, as the blood wasn't dry. When we arrived, the hood of her car was still warm. So, my guess is an hour or less."

Officer Casey nodded. "That makes sense. She called and left me a message about an hour ago. Said she was going to clean the house in case relatives came. We were on our way to meet her here. Instead, we got delayed by a call at a motel just south of here. You're going to want to be in on this as well. Found some more paintings that look just like the ones he had in here."

"What do you mean? Are they George's paintings?"

"We think so. The motel owner called us. Long story, but he found some paintings. We have them in our car and were going to contact you when this call came in. Let's go in and see what these officers found, and then we'll get the paintings."

Clark nodded to Marta and entered George's house with the officers. Two detectives met them at the bottom of the stairs. "Clark, why don't you take a look around to see if you notice anything different from last time?'

Clark went first into the den. "The small sketch that was on this easel is missing. It was signed as a Monet, but I'm not completely sure about that. I hadn't authenticated it yet. Everything else seems to be here. Let's go up to George's bedroom. That's where another valuable piece was, and I didn't take time to look once I saw Suzie."

All five made their way up the stairs and entered the bedroom. "Yeah, it's gone, too. Whoever was here this time knew what they wanted. Suzie must have been in the way. If it's the same thief, why didn't he take these the first time?"

"Maybe he got his paintings mixed up. Took the pretty ones and left the small ones. It would be easy to do if you're not up on your art." Officer Casey was walking through the bedroom, careful to avoid the bloodstained carpet.

"You may be right. Maybe he had no art knowledge whatsoever and was just following instructions from someone. Art is in the eye of the beholder, and maybe the thief liked pretty colors." Clark nodded to Officer Casey. "I think I'm done here, guys. Marta and I will calm Lucille and then go to the hospital to see how Suzie is doing."

"We'll let the detectives finish, lock up, and have a patrol come by here regularly for a few days. See if anything else happens here. You think the lady with the dog saw anything?"

"I don't know. She said she was just coming home from having her dog groomed and thought something was wrong, but she was a little rattled. I'll ask her again in case something comes to her.

"Oh, don't forget to give me the paintings from the motel. Tell me again what happened."

Chapter 21

Clark and Officers Casey and Street walked out together. "Sure. Apparently a guy checked in late at night and the clerk didn't run his credit card until the next day. When he did run it, it wasn't any good, so he contacted the owner. The owner went to the room to talk to him about the same time the maid was heading to that room. When they got there, they found the room had been trashed and the guy was gone. Owner checked to see who rented the room, and discovered the address and phone number the guy gave them was bogus; probably his name, too. The owner called us because of the bad credit card, the trashed room, and the paintings they found in the room. He figured they were stolen and wondered if the guy would come back to get them.

"We happened to be the ones responding, and when we saw the paintings we knew you'd want to be involved. They're right here in the car. You can take them with you."

"Did the motel owner get a good look at the guy who rented that room?"

"Nope. It was late, and he isn't real sure who checked him in. Of course, his security cameras aren't working, and his employees are tight lipped. The Ritz, it isn't. Let's talk to the lady with the dog. Will she be okay if we ask her some questions now, do you think?"

"Marta's been with her. Let's go see what she has to say."

The trio walked across the street to where Marta, Lucille, and Clyde sat. Marta stood up, still holding Clyde. "Clark, Lucille and I have been talking. She has seen a man come and go from here during the day sometimes. She thinks he does some work for George. He's not friendly at all, always wears a dark cap, and drives an older white sedan with a missing hubcap on the driver's side front wheel.

"The thing is, she's positive that car was sitting by the curb when she pulled into her driveway. By the time she took Clyde in the house and picked up his leash, the car was gone. She thinks it was about 20 minutes as Clyde wanted some water and a treat. She got her mail, put his leash on, grabbed a sweater for herself, and came out the front door. She has a good view of George's driveway and the street from her front door." Marta pointed to a house just up the hill.

Clark looked at Lucille. "That's a great observation, Lucille. Thank you. The officers will keep an eye out for a car that looks like the one you described."

Lucille smiled at Clark. "Is Suzie going to be okay? She is always so nice to me."

"We're not sure. Why don't Marta and I walk you and Clyde home, and then we'll head to the hospital? Did you and George ever talk about family and did you ever meet any of George's relatives?" The three of them started walking to Lucille's house. Clyde was now bouncing along on his leash, stopping to investigate every blade of grass.

"George mentioned his friends often. One time he told me he had a business partner, but the partner tried to swindle him, and George kicked him out. But, he never, ever talked about family. He would always tell me he was just a loner . . . didn't even have a dog like I do. I have no idea if he had any real family or not. What's going to happen to his house? George lived here a long time, you know."

"We aren't sure about the house. I guess we'll leave that up to the police. You've been a great help, Lucille. Now, Marta and I want to see how Suzie is doing."

They reached Lucille's door as she turned to Clark. "Wait. I remember George talked about a doctor at Stanford. I don't know if he meant a medical doctor or a different type of doctor, and I don't know if he meant the university or the medical center. I just know he mentioned him several times and referred to him as his adopted son. He was real proud of him."

"That's great, Lucille. You wouldn't happen to know his name, would you?"

"I sure do." Lucille smiled and then chuckled out loud. She stooped down and picked up her Pom. "Clyde. That's it."

Marta and Clark looked at each other, thinking Lucille may have just lost it.

"The first day I brought this little puppy home, George was out in his front yard. He looked at my new puppy and said his bright eyes reminded him of his adopted son, Clyde. He said I had to name this little guy Clyde. I was thinking more along the lines of Fluffy or Scooter. But, George kept calling him Clyde, and it stuck."

Chapter 22

Once at the hospital, Clark and Marta met with the surgeon as he came into the small waiting room. "I'm Doctor Wells. Officer Casey of the SFPD told me you are working on a case involving my patient. Are one or both of you related to the patient as well?"

Marta spoke first. "No, we are not related. We didn't even know her before all of this happened, but we knew the man who's home she cleaned. By the way, I'm Marta Swenson and this is Clark Moreno."

Nodding at Marta, the surgeon then looked at Clark. "Do I know you?"

"It's possible. I'm FBI and do some work for the SFPD as well. You may have seen me on another case."

"Probably. Well, since you're involved with the police case, let me tell you what we have. The patient presented with a gunshot wound to her left upper arm and chest area. Had the bullet been a little more to her right, it would have entered her heart and she would be in the morgue. As it is, it's still a serious wound, and she lost a lot of blood. She's lucky you found her as quickly as you did. And, she's lucky the shooter missed any vital organs. Her left arm is going to require physical therapy after reconstructive surgery, but she appears to be in good health, otherwise. Recovery shouldn't be too difficult for her, and she should regain her full and normal life. For now, she's sedated.

"You can see her but she won't know you're here. It would be better if you came back tomorrow. I can have the staff call you if there's any change."

"Thanks, Doctor Wells. We'll be in touch. You didn't happen to retrieve the bullet, did you?"

"As a matter of fact, it's on its way to the police lab now."

"Great. Another favor. Is it possible to not have any information about the patient get to any media? I'm sure Officer Casey mentioned this is an open case and we'd like the shooter to think the victim is deceased."

"He mentioned that, and her chart has a big 'NO MEDIA' on the front. That should work. Anything else?"

"No. Thanks again."

Dr. Wells looked at his phone as Marta and Clark left the small waiting room.

Chapter 23

"Marta, let's take the paintings Officer Street retrieved from the motel to your house as it's closer than my lab. You already have the other paintings there, and we can compare them. I'm wondering what their significance is in all of this. First, they're stolen. Then, they get left in a questionable motel. Now, it seems this thief took the valuable paintings. Same guy? Who knows?"

"I know. For some reason he decided George's paintings weren't what he wanted. Do you think he was smart enough to figure that out, or is someone else telling him what to take? Why else would he come back?"

Just as the elevator doors opened and Officers Casey and Street exited, Dr. Wells called out. "Mr. Moreno, could the two of you come back here a minute? My OR Tech has something you might like to give to the police. I've called them as well. Oh good, they're here, too. You can all take a look."

Dr. Wells motioned for the group to follow him. "Let's use this conference room." In his hand was a plastic bag. "One of my OR Techs found it when they were cleaning up the patient before surgery. We had to cut off her shirt, and she had some type of apron or cover over her shirt."

"She was cleaning a house at the time, so maybe it was what she used for supplies, rags, and things." Marta looked at the doctor.

"Yes. That makes sense. They said it had pockets and tied in the back like an apron. Anyway, this was in her pocket nearest the gunshot wound. It appears the corner might have deflected the bullet and in essence saved her life. It's a pretty solid book." He slid the plastic bag across the small table to them.

Officer Casey put on his gloves, opened the bag, and carefully slid the bloodied book out onto a mat on the table. Clark, also with his gloves on, sat next to him as they turned some pages with the tip of a pen.

After just a couple of minutes, Clark spoke to Officer Casey. "I'd really like to sit down and read this better. I realize you need to check it in as evidence first, but then I'd like for us to come to the station. Would that work?"

"Yeah, I don't see why not. Why don't you come down in an hour? We may be able to release it to you so you don't have to sit downtown and read it."

Clark was still looking at some pages. "Some entries are more than just journaling; they are drawings. I mean actual, working drawings. It's like he was designing something for someone. He has numbers, phone numbers, dimensions, and other combinations of numbers. I wonder if any of these coincide with the ones we found on his paintings."

"You found numbers on his paintings? Where? On the back?"

"Officer Casey, we think they are numbers. Remember those squiggly white lines? If you turn the canvas upside down, those lines start to look like numbers. Marta and I weren't sure what they meant, however. Now, we may have something to compare them to."

Officer Street's phone buzzed, and he left the room to take the call.

"We were just heading to Marta's place to compare all the paintings and see if we could come up with any numbers that made any sense. We have no idea what we're looking for, but figured it was a start now that we have all the paintings. By the way, did you have time to look for a doctor by the name of Clyde, yet?"

"Not yet. Why? Have you had any more thoughts on that?"

"I was going to contact Stanford and ask them to run a search on first names and then on last names of their medical doctors and their Ph.D. personnel. I don't know if they'll do that without a warrant, though."

"If you and Marta want to start there, I can work on getting a warrant."

Dr. Wells was still in the room, having taken a couple of phone calls, and now joined the conversation. "Did I hear you mention a Dr. Clyde from Stanford Medical Research Center? He's a colleague of mine, and he . . ."

Officer Street entered the small room, interrupting Dr. Wells. "We've got another victim. Close by. Gunshot wound to the head. White car, missing hubcap on driver's side. Could be our shooter."

Chapter 24

Officers Casey and Street left, taking the plastic bag with the journal in it. "We'll be in touch."

Marta turned back to Dr. Wells. "You started to say something about a Dr. Clyde. Do you have a few minutes? We'd like to know what you know about him."

"If it's who I'm thinking of, his real name is Clyde Janssen, but he goes by Dr. Clyde to all his friends and work colleagues. This man works in the medical research department at Stanford and has some amazing inventions. I think he works with different engineers and other people as well. Does that help?"

"Absolutely. We are trying to find out anything that relates to your patient, Suzie, and to the man she worked for. He was shot a few days ago in the same house where Suzie was shot. Marta and I haven't been able to track down a motive or any of George's relatives. He may be a key. Would you be able to introduce Marta and me to him?"

"Of course. Let me make a phone call, and I'll let you talk to him."

Dr. Wells placed the call while Clark left a message for Officer Casey. "We may have found Dr. Clyde at Stanford. Marta and I will meet with him and then let you know what we find out. In the meantime, we'll also look at George's paintings."

"Yes, they're here with me. Let me hand the phone to Clark." Dr. Wells handed the phone to Clark. "Dr. Clyde Janssen is on the phone. I don't know if he knows about George, though." Clark nodded and took the phone.

Hanging up after several minutes, Clark thanked Dr. Wells and told him and Marta they had an appointment with Dr. Clyde tomorrow afternoon. "Dr. Clyde is coming into The City for another appointment, and he will meet us at your home, Marta. Thanks so much, Dr. Wells, for introducing us. Maybe we'll catch a break about George's murder and Suzie's attempted murder. Please let us know when we can see Suzie, and we'll be back."

Turning to Marta, Clark said, "I am supposed to get to Venice for an ongoing investigation about some art forgery Interpol and the FBI are working on. I can put it off for a couple of days, but not much longer. When are you going back?"

"I specifically came here to meet George as he wasn't able to come to Venice for a few weeks. I really wanted to get his bracelet to Sam. Something about it is speaking to me. Maybe it's wishful thinking, but I keep wondering how it relates to Grandma's jewelry. It's like I have to close this circle. I don't know what it is about the bracelet, but it's on my mind. I was only planning on staying here for a week or less since I have a bunch of clients and work waiting for me in Venice. I thought I would come back to The City in a month and stay for several months. Why?"

"Let's talk to Dr. Clyde, see if we can help the SFPD wrap up anything, and head out together in a couple of days. We can follow up with Suzie from Venice. Are you flying back on Mario's plane?"

"Yes. It's still at the airport, waiting for me, as he doesn't need it right now. That way I can bring Shadow with me. He has all his shots and paperwork as long as I'm on a private plane. We're lucky Mario has the plane he does and that he lets me use it."

Marta looked at Dr. Wells and explained to him that Mario's grandfather and her grandmother were best friends growing up and that Mario and his wife live in Venice. "So, Mario refers to me as his extended family. And, that means I can use his private jet. I'm really spoiled."

"Nice to have those connections. I'll keep you both updated on Suzie's condition and a possible release date. Any idea if I need to have her family notified?"

"Dr. Wells, she told us she had no relatives. The police were going to check out her condo to see if there is anything they might find that would help us. We'll talk to you tomorrow morning."

Chapter 25

Stewart made it through security at San Francisco International Airport and was waiting to board the flight to Paris and then on to Venice. The bracelet was wrapped and tucked in his carry-on luggage. Bart's paintings and wine were labeled "Fragile" and in the checked containers Bart had provided. Stewart wasn't worried about them. As far as he was concerned, they were now Bart's problem. All he wanted was his money from Bart. No way was he going to tell him about the bracelet.

If the bracelet was worth half as much as he hoped based on its sparkle, he'd have a nice, fat wad of cash in his pocket. He wanted to take the bracelet out and look at it again, but the waiting area was filling up. He'd have to wait. "Lucky for me I saw it. Would have been a shame to let the cops have it." He meant to talk to himself, but in his excitement his voice carried to the man sitting next to him.

"Excuse me. Did you say the cops were coming?"

"No. No, I didn't. I was talking to myself about something else." Stewart picked up his bag and moved away from him. The man watched him walk over to another row of chairs, and he then walked to the opposite side of the waiting area. From there he pulled out his cell phone and pretended to fiddle with the buttons, while snapping a couple of photos of Stewart.

He sent Clark, the FBI, and Interpol a message with the photo attached. 'Run this face through your database and get back to me. Suspicious and jumpy. Talking about cops. Ian.'

Chapter 26

Stewart had time to send off a quick text to his friend in Venice before the flight attendants told him to shut down his electronics. He wanted to set up an appointment with some guy his friend knew so he could sell the bracelet. His friend had assured Stewart it was worth a serious amount of money based on the photo he sent.

Shutting off his phone, Stewart looked around the cabin. Families, tourists, and travelers not interested in him surrounded his seat. He thought to himself he wished he could have had an aisle seat, but this would have to do. He wanted to take out the bracelet and look at it in the lavatory. He'd really like to see it again. Did he have time? Maybe he should check his phone for any incoming emails or texts. He wanted to get his business done with Bart, sell the bracelet, pocket the money from both transactions, and get the heck out of there. He looked around the cabin again and tried to calm himself.

Bart made him nervous, really nervous. Especially after Bart told him to shoot that guy in the white car. He had no idea what the guy did to Bart. He only knew Bart was unhappy enough to have him shot. "Not the kind of guy I want to hang around with anymore. I'm done doing his dirty work." Shaking his head, he muttered softly to himself. "Now that I think about it, it bugs me that he always knows what's going on. I'm beginning to wonder if Bart has a connection here. Oh well, I'm outta here, and at least I got the bracelet out of the job. The best part is, Bart will never know it existed." Cautiously, he looked around the cabin again.

Even though the first announcement had already been made, Stewart turned on his phone and checked his emails and his texts. Nothing. He'd have to wait until they landed in Paris before he could check again. He quickly shut it off when he saw a flight attendant looking at him.

A few rows behind him, Ian checked his emails as well. Not hearing anything from Clark or Interpol, he put his electronics away and settled in his seat. When they were airborne, he'd talk to the head steward in this part of the cabin. He wanted to keep an eye on the jumpy passenger. Something wasn't quite right.

Chapter 27

Marta and Clark were listening as Dr. Clyde filled them in on what he knew about George. Clark was watching him closely. So far, they learned George was a brilliant inventor, quite wealthy, had a ruthless scoundrel of a partner at one time, loved good wine, and was on several research and development commissions around the country. "He never mentioned family. All I ever heard him say was that he was an only child and never married. We hit it off from the first time we met. I had just earned my Ph.D. and was asked to sit in on a meeting. We sat next to each other and became instant friends. He always introduced me as his adopted son, and I never corrected him. We had a special bond. I'm just so sorry it had . . ." He paused.

Regaining his composure, he shook his head as if to clear it out. "I still can't believe he is gone. Do you know who shot him?"

"Dr. Clyde, what makes . . ."

"Please call me Clyde."

"Okay. Clyde, I have some questions. Were you going to say something about the bond you had with him?"

"Uh, no." He looked away from Clark.

"Did George ever talk about his inventions?"

"Sure. All the time. We compared notes when we met for lunch or when I came here for dinner. We worked on changes, tweaking parts of them. Why?"

"So, did you see the drawings or any prototypes?"

"He didn't really have any real prototypes, but I saw his drawings all the time. We'd talk about them and make changes. First he would sketch in a black journal. Then, he would enlarge those onto graphed drawing paper. He kept those rolled up somewhere and brought them out when I was here. I assume he kept them in a safe place in his home. Why? Have you found anything like those?"

"We found the journal. Or, rather the woman who cleans found the journal. We're not sure where she found it, as she was shot and is still in the hospital. She had it on her when the police found her, and we haven't been able to talk to her yet. Right now it's at the police station as evidence. We'll go check it out later. But, no drawings. We've been through the house with a fine-toothed comb, too. I'm not sure where those drawings would be. Would he have had another place he stored them? How about at work? Did he have an office?"

"No. He always worked from home and would come into the lab only about once a month. I came here every week, and we'd work on things here. He was mostly in the designing and drawing phase, so he didn't really need much time in the lab. Did you find anything else missing?"

"Like what?"

"Oh, just things George had. He had a lot of nice things, you know." Clyde looked at his hands.

"Possibly some paintings. Did you ever see anything George painted?" Clark stood up, went into Marta's den where they had stacked the paintings, and brought them out. Lining them up against the wall, he asked Clyde. "Have you ever seen these before?"

"I think at least one was hanging in his den. I'm not sure which one, though. To me, they all look alike. Sorry."

"No worries. Do you remember where you saw it or if George said anything about it?"

"Yeah. He had just hung it and wanted me to see it. It was weird, though. He told me it was another key, but I didn't know what he was talking about. I remember making fun of it because it looked like something a six year old painted. He laughed and said that's what it was supposed to look like. I didn't think any more about it. How come there are so many of them?"

"Good question. We have no idea." Clark shook his head as he turned the first two upside down. His phone rang and he excused himself.

Clyde got up and picked up the one closest to him. "Wait. Are these numbers?"

"That's what Clark and I think. But, we have no idea of their order or what they mean. Do they mean something to you?"

"They could be. This one looks like a registration number George used to identify his work. His pieces all start with 14 and then a dash. Mine are 15 and two dashes. We could reference them that way." Clyde was turning all the paintings around until they resembled the numbers he was looking for. "Positive. These all start with 14, most have a dash, and I'm positive they refer to George's inventions. Why, that sly fox. He did this so no one else would know about the inventions, didn't he? These are the key he was talking about. No one would have a clue. Good job." Clyde smiled to himself.

"Clyde, you mentioned George's ex-partner was a scoundrel. Did you ever meet him?"

Marta watched as Clyde looked at his watch. "I've got to get to a meeting. I can be back in The City tomorrow, if you want to meet again. What's going to happen to these paintings?"

"I have no idea. Clark might have a better idea what will happen when the police are finished with them."

"The police. Oh, okay. Well, I've got to get going." With that Clyde headed toward the front door as Clark came back into the room.

"Marta, I . . ." His phone rang again, and he answered it as Clyde left.

Chapter 28

Clark hung up and turned to Marta. "The police have finished processing the murder that happened in the white car. It matches the description of the one Lucille saw at George's home, and the occupant's name is Franco Morris. He died of a single gunshot wound to the back of his head. No signs of a struggle. They found the chest that matches the photo Suzie had. It was in the car and empty, however. The shooter probably took the bracelet. No artwork or wine was found, either."

"Do the police think Franco Morris was the one who shot Suzie? Do they think he had the real paintings and that whoever shot him took them along with the bracelet? I know you didn't have time to verify their authenticity, but they would be quite valuable if they were real. Right?"

"Right. And, it appears George was wealthy enough to afford them, if indeed they were legit. As for Suzie, the police are comparing the handgun found on Franco's body to the bullet Dr. Wells retrieved from Suzie. If it's a match, then he definitely is the one who shot her. And, he probably stole the real artwork and possibly the wine.

"There are a few things that don't quite make sense yet, however. Was Franco in George's house more than once? If so, why didn't he steal the real artwork the first time? Why take wine?

Apparently, he took the chest with the bracelet and George's amateur paintings. Did he come back specifically to steal the real ones? He must have walked in on Suzie, or did he somehow know she was going to be there? It also makes me wonder if he acted alone or if he had a partner. And, what about the first guy who was shot at the same time as George?

"Who killed George? That guy or Franco? We know the bracelet is missing from Franco's car, and I guess we have to assume the shooter took the real artwork as well as the bracelet. Why?

The police are running ballistics on the bullet from his murder, but aren't hopeful of matching anything. They're also looking into his record and have sent his photo and file to Interpol as well. And, once again, we're back to questioning what George was doing in his wine cellar in the middle of the night. Are these incidents all connected?

"Speaking of Interpol, my friend Ian is working on an art forgery ring in Italy. I think I mentioned that to you. He sent me a photo from the airport. Take a look at this, and let me know if you've ever seen him." Clark pulled up the photo and showed it to Marta.

"No. Sorry. Does Ian think he's involved here or just in Italy? I'm not sure. He doesn't show up on any radar with either the FBI or Interpol. Ian just had a funny feeling about him. And, Ian's funny feelings are what saved his life and mine on a couple of occasions.

"On a different subject . . . There's something bothering me about Clyde." Clark's phone rang once more as he closed the photo. "It's Dr. Wells."

Hanging up a couple of minutes later, Clark motioned to Marta. "Suzie is sort of awake, but fading in and out. He thinks we should come and visit her, but he's not sure how much or how long we'll be able to talk to her just yet."

"After we see her, we could go to the police station and take another look at the journal she found at George's home. Maybe something will jump out at us. Oh, you started to say something about Clyde. What's up?"

"I don't know, and I can't put my finger on it. But, something is off. Did he seem jumpy and a little nervous to you?"

"Yeah, but we also just told him his friend was dead."

"Right. But, we didn't tell him George had been shot. How did he know that?"

Chapter 29

Sweating his way through the security checkpoint in Venice, Stewart wondered if he would have to answer any questions. Once his passport was stamped, he breathed a sigh of relief. Mentally carrying on a conversation with himself, he hovered around the baggage carousel and almost jumped out of his skin when the man next to him mistakenly picked up his carry-on bag that was sitting on the floor. "You have the wrong bag. That one's mine." He glared at the well-dressed traveler. Sheesh. Couldn't that guy even remember where he set his own bag?

Moving his bag closer to his feet, he'd have to keep a closer watch on it as he waited for Bart's shipping containers to come around the carousel. He didn't want the carry-on with his ticket to riches getting picked up by some stupid traveler. No way. Where are those containers? It seems like I've been here for a long time, he thought. Many passengers had already collected their bags and were headed out.

Finally, the containers arrived, and Stewart loaded them onto a cart. He knew he'd have to get a private water taxi instead of risking all this on the train. There were too many boxes and containers to keep track of. Finding the line for transportation, he muttered, "One more line and I can text Bart. Oh no, this guy again. Damn.

Why am I always running into him? He looks at me like I've done something wrong."

"Excuse me. Were you talking to me?" The well-dressed traveler smiled and gestured to Stewart's cart full of containers and bags. "You've got quite the load. Are you staying in Venice for a long time? It's a great city. Is this your first visit?"

Stewart gritted his teeth hoping he wasn't sweating profusely and tried to be pleasant. His answers came out curt. "I'm here on business." He looked away, hoping the man would leave him alone. It was not to be.

"Me, too. Great city for business. What business are you in? Antiques? You have quite a few containers that say 'Fragile.' Must be important items."

Wouldn't this guy ever leave him alone? Stewart glanced at the slowest moving line he had ever been in and replied to the man next to him. "Wow, this line sure moves slow." He hoped that would be enough of an answer. He really didn't want to get in any more conversations with the traveler. He just wanted to get to the water taxi . . . in a hurry.

The traveler nodded, smiled, and walked away.

"Thank goodness. Some people." Okay. Time to think. First, he would check into his hotel. Then, he had to call his contact about the bracelet. He didn't want to leave it alone for a minute. It was getting more valuable by the day in his mind. Finally, he would contact Bart and have the wine containers delivered to him. He'd deliver the paintings personally.

His phone rang, startling him. It was Bart. Damn. How did he know he was here? He'd ignore it for now. Maybe Bart would think he was still in the air.

Chapter 30

Ian Wells watched Stewart head to the water taxi. His text from his contact at the FBI identified Stewart as a small time thief who usually worked only in the US. His contact had no idea what Stewart would be doing in Italy. Especially with all those boxes. Ian had enough of a sixth sense to know something was up. The guy was as jumpy as the proverbial cat on the hot tin roof. He may be only a thief, but something was off.

In the meantime Ian contacted Interpol to see if they had any info on him here in Italy. Nothing, so far.

Clark hadn't gotten back to him yet, either. But, he knew Clark was busy in San Francisco. He decided to follow Stewart to his hotel and try to figure out what he was doing in Venice.

Showing his badge to the polizia, he told them he needed to catch up to a man that just left in a water taxi with a bunch of boxes and crates. Giving them the number on the boat, they quickly tracked down where it was going. Ian boarded a water taxi to take him to the same hotel and cancelled his reservation at the hotel where he was going to stay.

His phone rang. "Clark. Good to hear from you. Did you have a chance to look at the photo I sent?"

"Ian, both Marta and I looked at the man. Neither of us recognize him. We're headed to the hospital now and then to the police station where George's journal is. I'll show the photo to officers there. Maybe someone will recognize him."

"Well, I heard from the FBI who have him on their radar as just a small time thief in the US. Name's Stewart Jones. Or, at least that's one name he goes by. There may be others he uses. They don't know of anything he's doing or any time he's been here in Venice, though. He was jumpy as jumpy can get in the airport. He's traveling with some boxes marked 'Fragile.' It could be nothing but I really think there's a connection to my case. I found out where he's staying, and I'm booked in the same hotel. We'll see what happens. In the meantime, how soon do you think you can get here?"

"Marta and I will be there in a few days. We want to check on Suzie and see if George's journal leads us to anything before we leave. Okay?"

"Sure. Stay in touch. I'm at the hotel now. Talk to you later."

Chapter 31

Once at the hospital, Dr. Wells met them at the ICU. "Suzie is awake off and on. She's doing well, considering all she's been through, and we'll be able to move her to her own room later today. The police want to keep an officer by her door for at least a little while. That's okay with us. Let's go in and see if she is awake and can talk to you. Give her as much information as you can when you talk to her. It's less frustrating for her if she doesn't have to bring up any memories just in order to figure out who you are."

Marta smiled at the bandaged patient with her tubes dripping liquid and the machines whishing a rhythmic sound. Dr. Wells' description of her doing well wasn't the first thing Marta thought of when she saw her. Suzie's eyes were open.

"Suzie. It's Marta and Clark. Clark was the one who found you in George's home. We know you've been shot. But, Dr. Wells tells us you are doing well. We've had your car moved to your condo parking spot, so you don't have to worry about it."

Suzie was blinking as Marta was talking. Her eyes darted from Marta to Dr. Wells. With the tube recently removed from her throat, her speech was slightly hesitant, but there was a tablet lying on the table over her bed. She moved her hand out from under a series of tubes, picked up the pen, and wrote 'I know who shot me. It was the man George hired to hang paintings.'

Clark looked at the tablet. "Yes. You are correct. His name is Franco Morris. He was the one who stole George's paintings and the chest with the bracelet." Clark looked questioningly at Dr. Wells and he nodded. "Suzie, we have some other news. How are you feeling? Can you handle some more bad news?"

Frantically, Suzie nodded, her eyes getting big. "What?" The word came out scratchy.

"It's not about you. The man who shot you, Franco Morris, was killed later the same day. He was in his car, a car identified by George's neighbor, Lucille. There were no paintings in the car but the chest was there. However, it was empty. The police aren't yet sure who killed him."

Suzie scrawled on her tablet, 'where is bracelet?'

"We aren't sure yet. It could have been a random robbery, but the police are still investigating. Can I show you a photo of another man? I'd like to know if you've ever seen him."

When Suzie nodded, Clark pulled up the photo Ian had sent him, and showed it to Suzie. She shook her head and then wrote, 'who is he?'

"His name is Stewart Jones. He's not a nice guy. We have no idea at this point if he's connected or not. Another agent is checking him out. One more question. Do you know a man named Dr. Clyde Janssen?"

Suzie shook her head and sighed. It was obvious she was getting tired, and Dr. Wells stepped in. "I think that's enough for now."

"Last question, Dr. Wells. Suzie, do you remember picking up George's journal before you were shot? Do you remember where you found it?"

Suzie nodded as she wrote, 'It was in the back of a painting. I put it in my pocket. Where is it?"

Dr. Wells looked at her. "Suzie, it may have saved your life. It seems the corner deflected the bullet enough for it to miss your heart."

Clark took her hand. "We are going to look at it down at the police station. Do you have any idea why it was in the back of a painting? Have you ever seen it before?"

Talking as best as she could, Suzie whispered. "I have seen it a couple of times when he showed me his drawings. He said they were important and he had to keep them hidden so someone wouldn't find them. I don't know who. When I found it, it was kind of flattened and stuffed in the back of the canvas of one of his paintings. I think it was the last one he was working on. It wasn't finished yet."

Suzie let out another sigh, and Dr. Wells intervened once more. "Okay. That's enough for now. You can come back tomorrow."

Marta and Clark said their good-byes as Marta squeezed Suzie's hand. "Take care. You're doing great."

Chapter 32

Clark showed Ian's photo of Stewart to the officers and detectives at the police station. As with the FBI, their database showed him as just another thief but also as a some-time thug for hire. But, they didn't have anything currently connecting him to any murders or issues in San Francisco. They had also finished processing Franco's car and found only Franco's fingerprints. Officer Street had the chest. "If the shooter took the bracelet, then he must have worn gloves. The only prints on the chest were Franco's and some other ones, probably Mr. Hanson's. So, we're at a dead-end here. One bad guy is dead. Most likely, one more is on the loose. But, no one saw or heard anything . . . even in the middle of the day. Strange.

"But, we did have the journal photocopied for you and Marta. Thought it would be easier than trying to read it here. You can have this copy. The original will be held as evidence for a while and then given to his heirs, if there are any. Did you have a chance to talk to the other doctor, the one he referred to as his adopted son?"

"We did. He and George apparently got along real well, and he filled us in on how they worked on inventions, etc. We'll probably see some of George's drawings in this journal as Clyde said that's where they would start drawing ideas and things. Then, George would transfer them to larger graph paper. Clyde thought

George rolled each drawing up and kept it safe somewhere. He didn't know where."

Officer Casey nodded. "Do you trust this guy? Do you think he knew what George was working on? Was it important or highly sensitive? Could it have been the reason for the initial break-in or enough to try and kill the housecleaning lady?"

"I don't completely trust him, and I'm not sure why. He knows more than he's telling us. However, I didn't get the impression they worked on anything that was a huge secret or national security level. Did you, Marta?"

"No. Not really. But Clyde did make it sound like it was important enough that someone might want to steal it and take credit for inventing it. In fact, he mentioned that several times, now that I think about it. I think it was mostly medical devices, but I'm not positive. I also had the impression that Clyde didn't like George's former partner. It was like he had a deep hatred of him. But, I really don't know if he ever met him or if George just filled him with stories. Hard to tell. He started to say more, and then stopped. And, even though Clyde seems to think George had the drawings on paper and rolled up somewhere, we never found any rolled up drawings. Did you?"

Officer Street shook his head. "Nope. Nothing like that at all. And, no hidden rooms or closets or offices in the home, either. The home has been completely checked out. Do you think he had an office, a vault, or a safe deposit box somewhere else?"

Clark shook his head. "Clyde seemed to think George worked only at home on these. No office that Clyde knew about. And, they always discussed them at George's home. Never anywhere else.

"By the way, any heirs come forward, or did you find an attorney or a will? Clyde didn't think he had any relatives at all. Or, at least he never talked about any. And, they had been collaborating on inventions for several years. So, one would think George would have mentioned someone, if there were any relatives."

Once more both officers shook their heads. "Nothing at all. We'll keep you posted. We'll also need to call Dr. Clyde and talk to him. Anything else on your end?"

"Oh, one more thing Clyde mentioned. You know those white swishes on George's paintings we thought might be numbers? Clyde noticed them awfully quickly, and he's pretty sure they correspond to George's inventions and the numbers they assigned to their drawings. Marta and I are going to take another look at them. Not sure what good it will do if we can't find the actual drawings to match them to, though. Oh, has someone here read this journal?" Clark picked up their copy as he and Marta got ready to leave.

"Not yet. Do you think the house cleaner knows what's in it?"

"Not sure. Thanks for making the copy."

Chapter 33

Ian checked in at the hotel and spent some time talking to the hotel manager and concierge. He explained he was an Interpol agent in Venice on official business and was trying to keep track of another guest. He didn't want to alarm the guest or the hotel and was asking for their cooperation. When the concierge asked how he could help, Ian gave him his cell phone number. "Just in case the other guest does something strange. I could be of help to your local polizia. They have already helped me track him this far."

Nodding, they were both more than eager to keep an eye out for the questionable guest. "We don't need anything funny happening here."

Ian left and went to the temporary, local office that had been set up by the Rome Interpol office. With a working lab and art experts in place, they were dissecting several paintings of different sizes and by a variety of artists. Or at least, the supposed artists. Once he checked with the researchers, Ian noticed certain things that reminded him of the one he was previously working with in London.

Tomas, the head lab expert, welcomed him and showed Ian some paint chips from a 'Picasso.' "Look at these. We're getting close to tracking the paint. I think you'll find the canvases interesting, though. Make sure you stop over in that part of the lab. We can date those to a fairly recent time frame, probably no more than five years old. They're just made to look really old. Take a look over there and see what you think."

Ian walked to the far end of the lab where canvases of different sizes were being examined under microscopes and under different lights. All were being carefully dissected with tweezers and small, pointed knives as if surgery was being performed. One of the canvas experts looked up when Ian approached. "Ah. Good to see you again, Ian. Your eye will detect some things we found on this one. Take a look." He handed Ian some white gloves and pointed to the microscope.

Turning the knob carefully, Ian took his time looking at the fibers. "Okay. I've got a clear picture in my mind. What do I compare these to?"

"Take a look at this one now." The expert pointed to another microscope.

Ian took one look under the microscope and immediately looked at Tomas. "Wow. No comparison at all."

Tomas pointed to the second microscope. "We have just identified this as one Picasso used. The first canvas you looked at is from one of the Picasso paintings from a collector in Milan. At first inspection it originally dated to a more recent time. We have just verified that to be true. It is definitely a new canvas, not one Picasso would have had access to when he painted this. The collector knew something was off when he saw his same painting hanging in another gallery. He figured the gallery one was a fake, but it turns out, his was the fake. He supposedly had it authenticated before he bought it and everything. He's pissed, to say the least."

"So, lucky break for us? Or, does this just complicate things?"

"No, it's a break for us. We're getting closer to the forgers. Have you seen these small Monet drawings?" Tomas led Ian to another room where several people were looking at six smaller paintings. "These just surfaced. What do you notice at first glance?"

"Whoa. They all look alike. Or, at least quite similar. And, I really don't believe Monet did these. Right?"

"Exactly right on both observations."

"Where did you get these? I don't believe I've seen these before."

"They just came in from an auction house in Rome. Look what we found on the bottom of them. Numbers. Like they were painted in a series. Not at all Monet. The forger was getting cute or apparently thinks highly of his skills."

"Or, Tomas, maybe he's getting cocky."

"That's true, too. The funny thing is . . . numbers one and two are missing. These are all numbered three to eight. Did one and two not turn out like he wanted? Or, does someone else have them?"

Frowning to himself, Ian was trying to remember something.

"What's up, Ian? You look like something's wrong."

"There is. I just can't quite get it to surface. But, there's something about these that is bothering me. I mean, something more than the forgeries."

Chapter 34

Marta and Clark were sitting on her patio, reading the journal, drinking wine, and making a list to talk to Clyde about. He was due any minute.

Clark finished his pages, the first half of the journal. "Wow. Heavy stuff. It seems George's former partner was more than just a scoundrel, according to his early notes. He mentions the name Bart only one time, and he writes that he's not to be trusted, saying he fears the ex-partner is getting impatient with him. He wants them to sell incomplete drawings, and George refused. A couple of times George caught him doctoring something but he doesn't say what. George also caught him embezzling from their business account, and he writes that he was getting ready to take all the evidence to their attorney when the ex-partner attacked him. I'm not sure how he attacked. He says right after that the guy disappeared. George's attorney couldn't even find out where he went. He just disappeared.

"Then, he mentions him in connection with a medical device George had been working on. Some company in Germany bought the plans, but they were faulty. When George inquired, the company told them it was the ex-partner who sold the plans to them. He is positive his ex-partner is sabotaging his work, and he is very concerned about retaliation. His last entries here are about how he fears the guy is becoming more deranged. Those notes are written at the side, sort of like an afterthought. I wonder when they were written."

Clark looked up at Marta. "And, I'm still having conflicting thoughts about Clyde. I wonder if the SFPD found out anything on him. Let's be careful not to give out any information to him. What's in your half of his journal?"

"Well, there are lots of drawings, notes about ideas, conversations with Suzie, and lots of scribbles. In part, it reads like a diary. Like in your half, he writes some things along the side. These are in a different ink, so they may have been written much later than the original entry. He mentions important drawings and says they are safe, and no one will find them. One short note here says the ex-partner is not to be trusted and he's developing a series of keys to foil him. He doesn't say what he means by important or what the keys are. Do you suppose it's the same keys Clyde talked about? Then, this note is written sideways. He says he's figured out his keys. But, again, he doesn't say any more about the keys."

Marta turned to the last few pages. "Oh, good. He mentions his grandma's bracelet. I was hoping he would. He writes about where he was when his grandma gave it to him; apparently on her deathbed. He goes into detail about her health and then describes the bracelet. According to what is written here, it was an extremely important piece to her. He calls it her legacy to him and he is supposed to keep it safe forever, along with the other. What other? He has a bunch of notes, sort of like things or stories she told him. But, nothing is complete; it's jumbled. Then he stops and starts writing a list of questions he has for someone. I can't read the name, however, but he lists my name as a reference. Interesting. His last two pages are labeled 'ADMIN.' Let's see what he has in here. Maybe we'll discover something.

"This one is dated several years ago and I think we may have just found out some helpful information. He lists his attorney as Jack Jones and gives a phone number. No more about the bracelet, however. He also mentions the two small sketches. Weren't these the ones that were stolen? The ones that looked like Monet?"

"Yes. What does he say about them?" Clark moved closer to Marta as she laid the journal pages on the table in front of them.

"Look. He says he commissioned some paintings and will use them to put the scoundrel away for good. Is he talking about his partner again?"

"Well, he wouldn't have commissioned anything from Monet. I wish I'd had a chance to inspect those paintings. As for the scoundrel, it could be his former partner. But, I'm still wondering where he fits in this."

The doorbell rang, and Shadow scurried behind the sofa. Clyde apologized for being late. "I had a chance to talk to another professor and a research assistant from Stanford. They didn't know about George and were sorry to hear how he died. Everyone loved George and several mentioned he talked about a new type of mechanical arm for robot-guided surgeries. We had both been working on this for a while and George was close to perfecting it. It will improve the robots we use now.

"I asked if they had any idea where George kept his working drawings. No idea. No one ever knew George to bring work-in-progress to the lab . . . only completed plans. So, we still don't know where he kept his work. Sorry about that. And, I'd really like to find it."

Marta had shown Clyde to the patio and offered him a glass of Prosecco. "This is from my vineyard in Italy. Tell me what you think."

"It's refreshing and light. I like it. Thanks." Clyde looked at the pages lying on the table. "Is that George's journal? It looks like his scrawling handwriting. What does it say? Does he mention his partner? Does he mention me? Can I see it?"

Clark nodded. "Yes, it is his journal. The police made a copy for us as we thought maybe something would be here to help with his paintings and drawings. Why do you think he would mention the partner?"

"I don't know. Maybe he's still hanging around. I just thought maybe there would be something, that's all. Maybe he says who killed him."

Clark looked at Clyde and continued. "We'll let the police do their investigations of the murders. We're just trying to tie up some loose ends on George's paintings before Marta and I head to Venice. We'll leave them here at Marta's house for now. When the police have wrapped up the investigation, we'll figure out what to do with them."

"Are you guys leaving for Venice soon? Is there anything I can or should be doing?"

"Not really, Clyde. If they haven't already, the police will want to ask you a few questions. Oh, we did find a lawyer's name and number. On the off chance he's at his office, let's call him right now." Clark dialed the number George had listed, started a conversation, and proceeded to walk into the kitchen.

Marta asked Clyde if he ever saw George's family bracelet. "Yes. He showed it to me once. I think it's quite valuable." He went back to looking at George's journal.

Ten minutes later Clark came back to the patio with the bottle of Prosecco in hand. "You're not going to believe what I just found out."

Chapter 35

Marta took the bottle and poured. "We're all ears."

"Well, it seems George was in touch with his attorney quite recently. Because of his recent surgery and the fact that he wasn't supposed to lift anything, he hired a man to hang some paintings, move some boxes, and unload some supplies. According to his attorney, George had some reservations about this man. The man was Franco, as Suzie mentioned. The attorney figured George must have been really concerned as he mentioned Franco to him several different times. He's not sure why George didn't dismiss him. On another note, he changed his will within the last couple of months. The attorney will be getting in touch with Suzie as George left her a sizable amount of money and the chest from his desk. It's too bad it's empty, but since he only specified the chest in the will, maybe he didn't intend on giving her the bracelet. The attorney didn't know there was a bracelet."

Clark looked at Clyde. "He's also going to be getting in touch with you, Clyde."

"Me? Why? What's wrong?" Clyde fidgeted in his chair, drinking the remaining Prosecco in one gulp.

"Nothing is wrong, Clyde. The attorney will clarify, but I believe you will inherit some things from George. Including his house."

"Oh my. I never expected anything. Oh dear. Not good. His house . . . I can't believe it. Are you sure? Is this going to be public knowledge? Will anyone know about this? No one can know about this." Clyde was half mumbling as he stood up and paced the living room. Clark watched him with a quizzical look.

Marta watched Clyde as well and then turned to Clark. "Clark that's great, and it's fantastic for Clyde. But, it's hardly earth-shattering news. Is there more?"

Clark smiled at Marta. "Listen to this part. Remember the two sketches George mentioned in his journal? The ones where he said he commissioned them."

Marta nodded and Clyde stopped pacing. "If you mean the small one in the den, I asked him about that one once."

"What did he tell you?"

"Well, he said it was special, and that it was more like a trap than a piece of art. I distinctly remember he chuckled and said the rat would be taking the bait any day now. I didn't really ask anything more. But, you mentioned two of them. I only saw that one."

"Yes, there were two that were allegedly stolen by Franco the second time he was here. Then he was shot, and no paintings were found in his car. We assume the shooter took them. I'm wondering if the rat he was referring to was Franco. Possibly Franco admired them when he was in the house. But, why set a trap for Franco to steal them? Did he think he would catch him in the act? It's not quite adding up to what the attorney had to say."

"Was there more, Clark?"

"Yes, Marta there is. The attorney told me those two were forgeries."

Marta interrupted. "Forgeries? He knew he had forgeries?"

"Not only did he know he had forgeries. He specifically had them painted by a forger."

"What? Is that what he meant by commissioned? I'm confused." Marta was shaking her head and then picked up the pages from the journal. "Why would he do that? I still don't get it."

"The attorney didn't have any answers as to who painted them or why George wanted them. He only said George told him these two were special, and they would help put a really bad person away forever. He didn't tell the attorney anything more, and the attorney figured he would find out when the time was right. So, we have to assume the small Monet drawings were really not done by Monet. What we don't know is who did them, why George wanted them, and what the hell was he talking about when he told you, Clyde, that the rat would be taking the bait. He probably was talking about the same person when he told his attorney about the really bad person. But, who? It hardly seems like a small time thief like Franco would be worth George's trouble. So, who? And, why did George care about forgeries? Specifically, who is the really bad person?"

"Clark, you don't suppose these are in any way related to the forgeries in Italy, do you?"

"I've thought of that, Marta. It's a stretch, though, because we don't know if George ever went to Italy. I'll contact Ian, and then we need to get to Venice."

Clyde had been looking at the journal pages that were lying on the table. "Is it okay if I look at George's paintings one more time? I may be able to match them to the early drawings he has in here. Then, all we would have to do is find his actual drawings."

Marta stood up. "Let me bring them out into the living room, and we can look at them while Clark talks to Ian."

Chapter 36

Marta and Clyde had finished arranging George's paintings and matching them to his journal sketches when Clark came back into the room.

"I left Ian a voicemail. What did you two find?"

Clyde had been studying one of George's sketches from his journal and slapped his hand on his knee. "Now I know. He told me he was close. I can't believe it. We worked this one over so many times and the answer was always right in front of us. Terrific. Damn."

Marta and Clark had been watching Clyde as he moved around the living room, first holding up a painting, then comparing it to the journal. They looked at each other as Clyde continued to talk to himself. Shadow had moved away from Clyde three times already. Clearly Clyde was in another zone . . . one known only to him at the moment.

Abruptly he stopped and sat down. "I'm sorry. I must sound like a madman. I think I even scared your cat."

"Shadow's okay. Do you want to tell us what you're so excited about?" Marta picked up Shadow who looked at Clyde like he was going to start moving things again.

"Okay. Bear with me." Clyde lined up George's paintings on the floor in front of Marta's sofa, coffee table, and end table. "If

I'm right. And, I'm pretty sure I am." He looked at the journal and changed the order of two paintings. "Okay. Here goes. These first four paintings correspond directly to George's drawings he has here in his journal. They were ones he did before I met him. You can see these numbers in his squiggly white lines. I don't know if he was trying to make them look like birds, but it kind of seems that way to me. Sometimes the numbers aren't real obvious, but they're there. Especially, if you know what you're looking at. I can see what he was trying to do in concealing the numbers."

He picked up one of the paintings. "This one is his most famous. It has to do with a medical device he developed several years ago."

Marta nodded. "That was probably the one Suzie referenced that was used on her grandfather."

"It is. Anyway, now look at these two. The numbers are a little harder to figure out, but they do match some things George and I were working on together. Because I'm involved with these, they're easy for me to see. I have my drawings that show my work. We still don't have George's drawings. I know they exist, because I saw them . . . several times. I really wonder what he did with them. I'm sure he hid them for a reason. Probably didn't want me, or anyone, to get into trouble."

Clyde picked up the final painting. "Lastly, this one corresponds to a sketch he had started and then we both worked on. It's the mechanical arm I mentioned. We worked on it and worked on it. He must have redone the drawings lately and just didn't have a chance to show me. But, he has it all figured out. This is truly amazing. Boy, I wish we could find his actual drawings. Or, maybe I'm glad I don't have them."

Marta had picked up one of George's paintings and was looking at the front, the back, and the sides. "You don't suppose this canvas holds more of a clue than the numbers, do you? Is there anything under the paint?" She handed one to Clark.

Clark took out a small magnifying glass and a pair of tweezers and started picking at the back of the canvas. "Good guess, Marta. But, I think the answer is no. These seem to be cheap canvases and only one layer of paint. It would have been fantastic to find

George's drawings under the layers of paint. But, the paintings seem to be just what they are: brightly colored seascapes with white birds. Unless, the birds really are numbers and they represent the keys George referenced to you and in his journal. If that's the case, we might never know any more than we do right now. I'll ask his attorney again in case George referenced a place where he kept important documents or mentioned a key.

"Marta and I will head to Venice tomorrow morning, Clyde. We'll be in touch, and I know George's attorney will be contacting you as well. We should both be back in a couple of weeks at the latest. Keep us informed if you find out anything more about the drawings. Let me know if you think of anything else in the meantime."

"Will do. I should get back now. I have some papers that need to be turned in and some things to think about. None of this will be in the news, will it? I'd like to keep this all quiet. For George's sake, that is."

Chapter 37

Ian left the lab and saw he had two messages; one from Clark and one from the hotel concierge. He called the concierge back first and found out Stewart had requested a map showing the area near the Arsenale or the Arsenal. The concierge had given him a map and told him the best streets to use to get there. But, when the concierge asked if he could be of more service in finding a specific address, Stewart acted a little jumpy, took the map, and headed out. That was over an hour ago.

Ian thanked him, hopped on a vaporetto, and headed toward the Arsenal. He didn't think he'd find him, but it didn't hurt to wander around in that part of Venice just to see what might interest someone like Stewart. Was he meeting someone? Was he exchanging something or buying something? He'd bet his life that Stewart wasn't in Venice on vacation.

Ian strolled the streets and had just about exhausted every back street, every side alley, and every small bridge over another canal, when he saw a man exiting a non-descript doorway near a bar. Ian turned away, bent over as to tie his shoe, and watched as the man looked both ways and entered the bar. Ian carefully straightened up and moved to another bar down the street. This one was more crowded so Ian stood at the counter outside and ordered an Aperol Spritz. He could see the bar's doorway where Stewart entered, but Stewart wouldn't be able to see him.

After about forty minutes, Ian's drink was gone, and Stewart hadn't yet come out. Deciding it was too risky to take a look inside that bar, Ian decided he would come back later and check it out. He had the photo of Stewart on his phone and could show it to the bartender. He headed back to the hotel.

The concierge was just leaving as Ian entered. Clark thanked him for the information, asked him if he knew anything about the bar Stewart was in, and gave him some more Euros. Ian went up to his room and called Clark, leaving a voicemail. "Hey, I'm returning your call. Let me know what's going on. Talk to you later."

Then he sat down to Google the bar Stewart had entered.

The phone in his room rang. "Strange. Who knows I'm here?" Picking it up, the mechanical sounding voice on the other end said, "Don't let him get to her." Before he could answer or ask who the caller was talking about, he heard a dial tone.

Chapter 38

Clark, Marta, and Shadow landed in Venice. Mario had sent a private water taxi to pick them up directly from the airport terminal. "First class all the way. I can see how you get spoiled by this, Marta." Marta nodded as the water taxi pulled up to a dock area close to her home, the villa her grandmother left to her.

After everything was unloaded, Clark left to meet Ian at the lab, and Marta and Shadow settled in. Marta's housekeeper had left a note about a hand-delivered envelope on the kitchen counter, and Marta opened the weighty, elegant cream and gold envelope. A single sheet of embossed paper invited Marta to a party held by someone named Mr. B. Possa. "Shadow, who is this? Do I know him?" Marta noticed the R.S.V.P. date was past for the party to be held in two days. "Hmm. It might be fun. It doesn't say I can't bring a guest so I'll see if Clark wants to come. I hope it's not too inappropriate to respond late, saying I just returned from a trip. I'm curious who he is and how he knows me. You'll have to stay home, Shadow."

Meanwhile, Clark sent a text to Ian as he made his way to the lab. Ian greeted him at the doorway. "Glad you're here. We have some things we need your eyes to look at. Clark, I want you to meet Tomas who's heading up this investigation. By the way, did things get wrapped up in San Francisco?"

"Not completely. Close enough for right now, though. The police are still looking into the shooting death of the thief who stole George's paintings, and the housekeeper, Suzie, is out of Intensive Care." Clark turned toward Tomas as they shook hands.

"Clark, I've heard good things about you. Thanks for coming. Sorry to take you away from whatever you were working on in San Francisco." The three men walked to the Picasso that was now being totally dissected. Clark put on his gloves as he bent over to get a better look.

"It's good; isn't it?"

"Yeah. As far as forgeries go, this one could fool a lot of people. And it did."

"Why and how did someone have doubts about its authenticity?"

"The owner, who had it authenticated and had what he thought was the provenance, saw this very same painting in a gallery in Spain. Originally, he thought the poor gallery had been duped. That's when he decided to speak to the gallery owner and ask about the verification. As he's hearing from their specialists, he's getting a bad feeling about his painting. He called in another specialist who told him his painting was a fake and so was his provenance. That expert called us. This is that painting, which was painted quite recently. And, not by Picasso."

"Any idea where he bought it or who originally verified it for him?"

"None. Unfortunately, when he found his bill of sale, the name of the seller and the verifier were both fake as well. Definitely, the work of an expert in the business of selling forgeries. We do not believe this was a fluke or one-time deal. We're kind of at a dead-end on this one until others surface or until our lab finds that one clue buried in the paint.

"But, I want you to see some things we recently had come to the lab." Tomas led them to the room with the small paintings. Several lab workers were in various work stages.

"These came from a respectable auction house in Rome. The owner knew right away they were fake. But, no one at the house knew where they came from. They were just in a box that was sitting in the back room. No idea how long they had been there, even though they carefully catalog every shipment in and out. There are some things you'll notice right away, and I want to . . ."

"Whoa." Clark interrupted Tomas. "Sorry to interrupt. But, I know these. Or, at least two very similar to these." Clark walked to the one closest to him and carefully picked it up off the easel.

Ian and Tomas looked at Clark. "What do you mean, you know these? Have you seen them before?" Ian looked at Clark as he studied the one in his hand.

Setting the first painting back, Clark picked up a second one. "I'm positive. Damn. I wish I had taken more time to get a better look."

"Okay, Clark. Where have you seen these, and what do you know about them?"

"I've seen two just like these. In San Francisco. Associated with the murders and break-in I was consulting on with the SFPD and the FBI. Recently, they were stolen from the murder victim."

Chapter 39

Explaining the situation to Tomas and Ian, Clark nodded his head. "Yeah. These are by the same person. I didn't have time to look at the bottoms to see if there were any numbers like these. But, everything is a match. I'd bet on it."

Ian excused himself to take a phone call and came back a couple of minutes later. "I have to make a quick trip to a bar. Remember the photo I sent you, Clark, of the guy on the plane? Something's just not right about him, and I have a lead on where he's headed. It's a bar not far from here. Want to come along?"

They headed to the same area of Venice Ian had followed Stewart to before. "Ian, how do you know where he's headed?"

"The concierge is helping me. He doesn't want any trouble for their hotel. Okay. We're here. Let's hang around for a few minutes. We probably beat him here as we were a lot closer than he was if he was coming from the hotel."

Standing at an outdoor table with their coffee, it wasn't long before Ian spotted Stewart walking toward them. "I'm going to go inside as I don't want him to notice me. Watch to see where he goes." Clark nodded, pulled a guidebook out of his pocket, and pretended to read it. Stewart passed within a few feet and continued on to the same bar he was in the other day. Another man came from the opposite direction and entered the same bar. Clark motioned for Ian, and they followed him.

"There are two men. I have no idea if they are together or if they just happened to arrive at the same time. What do you want me to do, Ian?"

"Let's just watch for a few minutes. You might have to go in."

Less than 10 minutes later, Stewart came out and quickly moved past Clark and Ian, not giving them a second glance. The other man followed shortly, talking excitedly on a cell phone and moving at a fast pace. Clark was able to figure out a few words of his conversation as he walked past, and they discreetly followed.

Once he was out of earshot, Clark asked Ian if he could get any more of the conversation. "I'm pretty sure he was talking about jewelry. Is that what you heard?"

"Yeah. Specifically a jeweled bracelet."

"He also said it was too much of a coincidence to not be real. Whatever he meant by that. And, he mentioned that he would be at the shop in 20 minutes. Anything else you heard?"

"No. That was about it. I don't think we're going to be able to catch up to him. He's moving fast. I wonder what the connection is between the two men."

"Clark, I have no idea. Right now, I'm going to head back to the hotel and talk to the concierge. How about you?"

"I'm going to Marta's. We'll be in touch."

Chapter 40

Stewart was so excited he could hardly keep his feet on the ground. "Rich. I'm going to be rich. I might even tell Bart where he can go. Who needs him anymore? Not me, that's for sure." The meeting with the jeweler's assistant had gone better than he dared to hope. He had a small down payment in one pocket, the bracelet in another pocket, a promise of big money, and a meeting set for later. "I'm going to swing by the hotel and then head to the meeting. After that, I'm dropping the paintings at Bart's office. I might even book a flight out of here for tonight. The further away from Bart, the better."

His phone rang, and he noticed it was Bart. "Damn, the man must be psychic." But, he had to answer it, as he hadn't talked to him since he landed.

"Hey there, Bart. How are . . ." He was cut off in mid-sentence.

"Listen to me and listen good. I know you're in Venice. The plane landed over three hours ago. The cartons of wine arrived already. Apparently, you still have the paintings, and I'm not sure why. I expect you in my office in half an hour with them."

The call ended abruptly, and Stewart was left listening to silence. "Damn right I still have the paintings. They are my insurance. What does he think I am? Some errand boy he can just order around? Half an hour? That means I need to let Pedro know I'll be late. Damn. Bart's messing with my schedule." He shoved the phone in his pocket.

Back at the hotel, he took the paintings out of their box and stuffed them in his satchel. Slinging it over his arm, he headed out and didn't notice as Ian watched him from the lobby.

Ian nodded to the concierge and followed Stewart out the door.

Chapter 41

Marta showed Clark the invitation, asking if he knew anyone by the name of B. Possa.

"Not at all. But, then I don't live here like your grandmother did. Maybe this person was someone related to a friend of hers."

"I don't think so. That would have been too long ago. I Googled the name and came up with a disturbing find. The only B. Possa I could find in Venice or in Italy is a Bart Possa. Does that name ring any bells? And, didn't we read George's former partner's name was Bart? But, I don't recall a last name, do you?"

"Not at all. And, I don't like the coincidence."

"Well, there's more. Guess what he does? He's an art collector and an inventor, originally from California. How's that for an even stranger coincidence?"

"Whoa. Not good at all. I'm going to call George's attorney to see if he knows the last name of George's former partner. By the way, what's the party for?"

"The invitation says he just acquired two new paintings for his extensive collection and wants to share them by having a party. Sounds pretty full of himself, if you ask me."

Clark nodded to Marta in agreement as he made the call to George's attorney. "George told him the partner's name was Bart

Astor. I still think we have too many factors here for us not to be concerned. Are we going to the party?"

"Absolutely. We have to, now."

"Good. I'm also going to call Ian and fill him in on this development. He may want to figure out how to get invited as well."

Clark left a voicemail for Ian. "That's odd. He said he was going to the hotel. He must have something else going on."

Chapter 42

Ian stayed behind Stewart as he stopped at a building, probably a former palace, just off the Grand Canal. With its gleaming white marble façade and gilded doors, he wasn't sure if it was a residence or something more office oriented. Ian stayed around the corner as Stewart looked up and down the street. When he felt the phone vibrate in his pocket, he didn't take time to see who it was. Stewart had stopped and looked around several times, and Ian didn't want him to see him.

Ornate doors at street level were typical of residences and offices in Venice. Ian positioned himself to get a glance inside as Stewart rang the bell and they opened. Again typical, the first floor was nothing more than an entrance with stairs. Water issues and flooding demanded you didn't live or have anything valuable on the ground floor. All Ian could see were gleaming marble-like floors that matched the outside walls before a uniformed man closed the doors. By the looks of the man, he was not your ordinary butler. With a chest that looked like a linebacker, Ian knew he wouldn't want to mess with him. Looking up, he could see there were four floors above. Still not sure if it was a residence, he decided to wait until Stewart came out. His phone buzzed again.

Two messages. The first from Clark, telling him about a Bart Possa. Immediately, he ran that name through his database, then forwarded it to the FBI and Interpol. He received an immediate response from Tomas and made a call to him.

"What's up, Tomas? You said this was urgent."

"The name Bart Possa. We've been trying to get to him, as his name has been associated with some questionable art dealings in Rome. We always get stonewalled, as if he is protected somehow. What do you know about him?"

Ian related what Clark had told him. Then, he filled Tomas in on Stewart's visit to this palace. "I have no idea what he's doing. But, something is still off about this guy."

"Ian, we need someone to act as a buyer and meet with Bart Possa. Hopefully, we could track some of his buying and selling. This party might be a great way to get that done. Can you pull it off?"

"If Possa is in any way protected, I might be recognized. What about Clark. Or, for that matter, what about Clark and Marta?"

"That's a better idea, I think. When did you say the party was?"

"Soon, I think. Why don't all of us meet and form a plan? How about later today at your office? Wait. Gotta go. Stewart is coming out. And, he doesn't have his large satchel. Strange. I'll call you in a few."

Ian stepped back into the doorway and hunched down so Stewart wouldn't notice him. When it was clear, he followed Stewart as he boarded another vaporetto and headed across the canal.

After a couple of stops, Stewart disembarked, headed over two small bridges across canals, and entered a doorway. The sign overhead read 'Jeweler.' It was obvious Stewart was nervous by the way he wandered around the shop, looking over his shoulder often, and almost jumping out of his skin whenever someone else entered the shop. Ian watched from just outside, pulling a cap out of his pocket and wearing it down over his face. He had also turned up the collar on his shirt and removed his jacket.

A few minutes later a man came from the back and greeted Stewart, motioning him to sit down at the table toward the back of the shop. Ian couldn't see what they were doing, and since he didn't want to risk being identified by Stewart, he stayed outside. After several minutes, Stewart exited and headed the opposite direction from Ian.

Ian entered the shop, looking for the man who had been with Stewart. When he didn't see him, he asked the young man at the counter if he could meet with the shop owner.

"I am Sam, the shop owner. May I help you?" A man came from a curtained area at the back.

Discretely, Ian pulled out his Interpol credentials. "There was a man in here a few minutes ago who is of concern to the FBI, Interpol, and your polizia. What can you tell me about him?"

"Well, that makes me feel better. The only thing better would be if he was wanted by your San Francisco city police. Let's go in my office and chat."

Chapter 43

"Okay, Sam, now you have my attention. Why would you mention San Francisco?"

Taking a deep breath, Sam folded his hands on the table. "Where do I start?"

"How about with what this man was doing here?"

"No. I need to start before that. Many years before that. You need to have the entire picture." Sam began. "About three years ago, Mario, a friend, put me in touch with a lady by the name of Marta Swenson when her grandmother died and left her some amazing pieces of jewelry. Marta lived in San Francisco. Turns out Marta's grandmother's family was royalty, and the jewelry was beyond valuable, historically as well as monetarily."

Ian was nodding and interrupted. "Marta Swenson, friend of Clark Moreno?"

"Yes. Do you know them?"

"Yes. Go on."

"Anyway, there were some murders and robberies, all somehow associated with the jewelry and Marta's family. But, it was finally all straightened out, and Marta discovered the history of her grandmother's jewelry, tiara, coins, and other items that had been left to her. Most of the pieces are now on loan to a museum here. Fast forward to a few days ago, when Pedro, my assistant, was made aware of an astonishing bracelet. You see, Pedro has some interesting friends, and one of them deals in some less than above board transactions. This friend got all excited and showed Pedro a photo of a bracelet. I believe the friend wanted Pedro to sell it and then give him a cut of the sale. Pedro came to me with the photo.

"That's when I knew something wasn't quite right."

"What do you mean, not quite right?"

"Well, for one thing, the story told to Pedro was that this guy just found the bracelet. Found it. Not believable, to say the least, considering the bracelet. Second, even in the photo I could tell it matched Marta's grandmother's necklace identically. So, Pedro and I decided he had to meet the man with the bracelet. He would tell him he had to bring it to his boss so he could authenticate it and place a value on it. The boss, me, was the one with the money and would be the one paying him for it. Instead, the man decided he didn't want Pedro to have it, even though we gave him a small down payment. He wanted to bring the bracelet himself. That's what he was doing in my shop today. I told him I needed it for two or three days to make sure it was genuine. He didn't like it, but I threw out a huge dollar amount, and he begrudgingly agreed. In fact, I was just getting ready to call Clark and Marta."

"Well, let me save you the trouble. They are both here at her villa. They could be here in about half an hour."

"Great. You call them, and I'll get the bracelet out of the safe."

Within twenty minutes they all entered Sam's shop and headed to his office at the back. "Sam, it is so good to see you again. I'm nervous and excited. I keep hoping it may be related to Grandma. And, I have so many questions." Marta hugged Sam.

"Marta, good to see you as well. Let's all sit down and start from the beginning. I'd like to understand where this came from."

Everyone filled Sam in on what they knew about the bracelet. Marta told of meeting George and finding out he had a bracelet his grandmother left to him. Clark filled Sam in on George's murder, Suzie's attempted murder, and the thefts. Ian finished the story with how and why he followed Stewart to the bar and then to Sam's shop. Pedro confirmed he was the one Stewart met with at that bar.

Ian nodded. "I thought that was you. And, I need to point out . . . this wasn't Stewart's first stop today. He stopped at this address, where he left his satchel." When Ian mentioned the address, Marta interrupted.

"That's where the party is, isn't it Clark?"

"Yeah, it is. Was it a home or a museum?"

This time Sam interjected. "It's the home of a very wealthy, almost reclusive, art collector. There is no lack of rumors surrounding the owner, all the way from stealing to forgery to unscrupulous dealings to bribing law enforcement. What party?"

"We have an invitation to a party there tomorrow night. The invitation says he is showcasing his latest collection. Very highbrow and apparently exclusive. I have no idea how my name ended up on his guest list, but Clark and I are going."

Ian motioned to Clark. "There's one more thing. You, Marta, and I need to meet with Tomas. Interpol has an undercover assignment for the two of you that concerns that person and his party. We'll go there next."

As Ian was talking, Sam was unwrapping a green, velvet pouch. All eyes were on the pouch, especially Marta's, as he carefully laid the bracelet on the black cloth in front of him.

Marta could hear herself gasp. "Oh. My. God. It's a match, isn't it? Sam, what do we have? I really can't believe my eyes." She picked up the bracelet, which sparkled in the light. "Oh, Grandma."

Chapter 44

Stewart took his time going back to the hotel. He couldn't shake the feeling he was being followed.

"It would be just like Bart to have someone follow me. I'm going to show him I'm just having a good time in Venice. Nothing more, now that the paintings have been delivered. I can't wait to get the bracelet sold, the money in my pocket, and a ticket out of here. I hoped it was going to be today, but guess I'll have to wait a couple of days. That's okay. Might as well enjoy myself."

After asking the hotel concierge where he should go for drinks before dinner, he changed clothes and headed across the canal. His phone rang, and he swore. "Damn. What the hell does he want now?"

Answering it, "Hello, Bart. What can I do for you?"

Standing on the street, Stewart was nodding, trying to speak, nodding some more, and finally answering. "Yeah. I'll be there."

He entered the bar, ordered a Spritz, drank it in two gulps, and ordered another one. If the waiter noticed, he didn't say a thing.

Talking softly to himself, "Damn. I can't get away from this guy. At least he says this will be the last thing he wants me to do. And, he is paying nicely. Since I have to wait for the other guy to pay me for the bracelet anyway, I might as well go make some more money off Bart. It's a party. All he wants me to do is stand around and watch people. How hard can that be? Sounds like easy money to me."

Stewart finished his drink, left the bar, and headed back toward the hotel.

Chapter 45

Sam was inspecting the bracelet as everyone else watched in total silence. After a few minutes, Sam put down his loupe, pulled up an image on his computer, and made some notes.

"Marta, from my previous notes and measurements from your grandmother's necklace, I'd say this is a match. The quality of the stones, their size, clarity, everything matches as closely as possible. If these two weren't initially made as part of a matched set, I'll eat my desk."

Everyone smiled. Marta stood up. "Sam, what does this mean? Where do you think George got it? Did his grandma really leave it to him? Why? What do we do? How is this connected to Grandma? I wish I could have talked more to George about it. And . . . why?" She stopped pacing and looked at Sam.

"I can't answer most of those, Marta. Since George told you his grandmother left it to him, that's probably where he got it. Before that, how and why she had it, we'll never know. We already have your grandmother's history and her relationship to her royal family. We can ask if the museum curator knows any more about the jewels from that family. All that would do, however, is prove they came from the same family. Does that mean George's grandmother was related to yours, Marta? Possibly. But, again, it's all supposition unless we can find documents supporting that.

"I'll spend some time with the curator, and we will look into this history some more. In the meantime, it will stay in my store safe, if that's okay with everyone."

Ian nodded. "I think that's best for now. That is, if your safe is truly safe."

"It is. But, I have a question. What do either Pedro or I tell the man who brought it here? What was his name again?"

"It's Stewart Jones, according to his record in the States. Clark, what do we want to use as a story?"

Clark smiled. "I was thinking about that. Pedro, you need to simply say your boss, Sam, is making sure he does a thorough inspection. Tell Stewart that Sam doesn't want to shortchange him. If Stewart is in this for the money, that should appease him. Is he coming back here, or are you to contact him?"

"I'm supposed to leave a message at his hotel that his package is ready for pickup. That means I have the money to give him. That's what he arranged."

"Good. You won't have to deal with him in person. But, at some point we need to pick him up. Or, have Interpol pick him up, with the cooperation of the Venice polizia. Let's wait a day or two on that. Okay? After all, he may do something stupid in the meantime." Ian looked at everyone. "Now, Clark, Marta, and I need to get to Tomas' lab."

Marta took one more look at the bracelet. "I wish I knew more." She picked up the bracelet, looked at it. "Sam, do you think Grandma had more pieces?"

*C*hapter 46

The plan was developed; stories were created; they had rehearsed it, and everything was in place. Marta had called in a late R.S.V.P. to the party, apologizing and asking if it was okay to bring her art-collector guest from America, a Clark Morris. Credentials were being made to show Clark Morris as an eccentric art collector from San Diego who had unlimited money to spend and wanted something new for his collection. He was also portrayed as ruthless and didn't care how he acquired his artwork.

Since Bart Possa was a person of interest to Interpol, the Venice police, and the FBI, this would be a good way to see if he really had knowledge of or was involved in any forgeries. Clark mentioned the name George's lawyer told him, Bart Astor, as George's former partner. No one, including Tomas, and contacts at Interpol and the FBI had heard that name.

"I still think there's got to be some connection between the two. And, there has to be something connecting all this to George. I'm just not sure what it is yet. Maybe Marta and I will find out tomorrow night."

"Clark, your instincts are always good. You're probably right about the connections. We just haven't put all the pieces into play yet. Keep in mind, tomorrow night is more about getting Mr. Possa for the forgeries here. If they lead us to San Francisco, that'll be great. If not, we'll have to figure a different angle there. Now, you and Marta have your stories down pat? Any ID you need will be delivered to Marta's by tomorrow. Your background and anything anyone would look up on you is already in place. You do have a tux, don't you? You need to look wealthy."

"I'm also eccentric. Remember? That gives me some leeway on my actions and questions."

"Right you are. Just be careful. From what Interpol knows about this guy, he can be dangerous. Apparently, his security people are thugs. We don't want anything happening to either one of you. Marta, this lipstick tube is a signaling device. If he has security, it will go through as lipstick. See? But, once you wind it all the way out, it becomes a signal. We'll know something's wrong if that happens. Okay?"

Marta nodded and put it in her purse. "I still wonder why he invited me in the first place. Do you think he knows me?"

"At this point, we have no idea, but we're working on that. Remember to stick by Clark's side for a while. Then, mingle and keep your eyes and ears open. If he has paintings or artwork on the walls, pretend an interest and try to remember what they are. Pay attention to what he calls his newest acquisitions. Remember who the artist is and get a good first impression of the piece. Ask other interested parties what they think of that piece. You'll do fine.

"I don't want you to stay more than an hour or slightly more. Clark, tell him what you want and move on. Make him come to you. I don't need to tell you how to do this. You're seasoned. It's best if he thinks you are going back to San Diego real soon. Okay with everything so far?" Ian looked at Clark and Marta.

He knew he wouldn't have to worry about Clark. He had done this type of thing hundreds of times. Marta was new at this, and he hoped she wouldn't give anything away with a look of surprise or stumble on an answer. With this short notice, they'd have to hope for the best.

Chapter 47

Marta was dressed, her new lipstick in her purse, and only slightly nervous. When her grandma left her a jewelry box filled with an assortment of valuable stones and exquisite, finished pieces of jewelry, she had Sam use three of the smaller, but still magnificent stones, to create an elegant necklace. When she wore it, she was reminded of her grandma. The distinctive, faceted, clear, teal blue stones matched her gown perfectly. It also matched the stones in the royal necklace and tiara from her grandma . . . and now the newfound bracelet.

"Clark, I hope I don't do something stupid." She fingered her necklace as she looked in the mirror.

Clark emerged from the bedroom in his tux, and Marta whistled. "Wow. You look dashing and not at all eccentric. Agent 007 has a new rival."

"Wow, yourself. You look fantastic. Is that Grandma's necklace? It suits you."

"Thanks. It's the one I had Sam make for me, and I wear it on special occasions. I really don't wear it as often as I like, though. Maybe it will bring us luck tonight. Are these new cufflinks?" She lightly touched the large square black and silver cufflinks on Clark's sleeves.

"Yep. They're not normal cufflinks. I should be able to get some halfway decent photos with these babies. Now, if I'm talking to Bart, remember to mingle, keep your ears and eyes open without appearing to look around. We need to be out of there in an hour, and we have our excuse. We need to leave about 8:30, or shortly thereafter, to make it to our dinner reservations, which are at 9:00. That should be about right, and it won't look like we're trying to escape. Okay?"

Ian had arranged for a private water taxi to meet them near Marta's palace and take them to the party. As the driver assisted Marta into the wooden boat, he uttered, "Good evening."

Marta's head snapped up. "My, what a fine captain. Hopefully, you know how to drive a boat!"

Ian chuckled. "We'll see."

Marta and Clark approached the same ornate doors Stewart had entered only yesterday. "Wow. Impressive doors. If the rest is as grand, we're in for a treat." Marta took her invitation from her purse and handed it to the doorman, who easily could have played on any NFL team.

To Clark, it was obvious by the bulge at his side that he was heavily armed.

As they made their way up to the first floor from the ground floor, Marta mumbled to Clark. "I hope I'm dressed appropriately. I don't want to create any undue attention." Clark didn't have time to respond as they stepped into a large foyer; a gigantic chandelier overhead reflected hundreds of light prisms in the mirrored walls and endless windows. Soft music played in the background while a tuxedoed, handsome, older man approached them, kissed Marta's cheek, and shook Clark's hand.

"You are Marta Swenson from San Francisco, correct? And, your guest is Clark Morris. Am I correct on that as well?" Bart was staring at Marta's necklace.

Clark took the lead. "You are exactly correct. You must be our gracious host, Mr. Bart Possa."

Bart chuckled. "Please call me Bart. All my friends do. And, we have friends in common." His eyes moved for only a split second to Clark's face, then immediately back to Marta's necklace.

"My dear, what a lovely necklace. Are those gemstones family heirlooms? I really must see it. In fact, sometime I'd like to inspect it better as old jewelry is a hobby of mine. It suits you." He turned to Clark. "Where are you from Mr. Morris?"

Clark put his arm around Marta. "Please call me Clark. I'm from San Diego. Just visiting my dear friend, Marta, for a couple of days. Had some time in between business dealings and wanted to check out some things in Venice. I'm always looking to add to my collection."

Marta addressed Bart. "Clark collects art, and I thought it would be a perfect party for him to attend. I've heard you have quite the collection. I hope you don't mind."

"Not at all, my dear. I love meeting new collectors. Tell me, Clark, what do you collect? Maybe I can give you some contacts while you're here in Venice. How long did you say you were staying?"

"I can only be here a couple more days. I'm really into Picasso. Have quite the collection back home. I certainly could add a new piece, considering I just completed a deal that left me with some extra spending money." Clark looked around the room. "Looks like you have almost as many as I do."

Bart gritted his teeth while still smiling. "I probably have more. I move my collections around from time to time, so these are not all I own. But, lucky for you I recently came into a Picasso that I really don't have room for right now. Would you be interested in seeing it?"

Marta moved to the side. "If you gentlemen will excuse me, I'd like to get a glass of wine and look around. I'll let you talk business."

"Of course, my dear." Bart motioned to the waiter to bring Marta a glass of wine. "Please enjoy yourself while we visit some more about helping your friend add to his collection. And, then you really must show me your necklace."

Smiling, Marta accepted the wine and wandered around the large room. Strategically placed windows offered perfect views of the Grand Canal. Two long walls were adorned with artwork, individually illuminated as if they were in a museum or art gallery.

"Impressive." She spoke to no one in particular. At least 20 people mingled around, several grouped in front of one painting. Wandering to that one, she noticed it was a Monet. She listened for a while, taking mental notes as others commented on it, and then moved on.

As she turned to look at another piece, a man caught her eye. He wasn't looking at her, but rather at Clark and Bart. He was the man Ian was following. He was the man who had George's bracelet.

Chapter 48

Stewart had to admit. This wasn't a bad gig. And, Bart was paying him to be here. He just wasn't sure what he was supposed to be looking at or for. Everyone looked like they belonged at a high class party, nothing unusual at all. No one was trying to steal any of Bart's paintings. Oh well. He'd have another glass of wine and keep moving. Looking toward Bart, he saw he was in deep conversation with another man.

As he watched, they moved over to Bart's hidden doorway and left the main room. "Wonder what that was all about?" He mumbled to himself and picked up another glass of wine. "Have to say, he has good taste in wine."

Marta also watched as Clark and Bart disappeared into the hidden doorway. Deciding Clark could take care of himself, she listened as several people had interesting comments about Bart. Chuckling to herself, she then decided to make small talk with the man Ian had been following. She wished she had a camera. Picking up another glass of wine, she set her half full one on a tray, and moved slowly around the room looking at the artwork. "Excuse me. Do you like this one?" Stewart was on her right, not really looking at anything.

Abruptly, he turned to walk away. There was no way he was going to get in any discussion with someone about art. They would know he didn't have a clue. Bart told him to watch, not talk to people.

"I'm sorry. I didn't mean to startle you. I was just thinking I don't really like this one, and I wondered if anyone else felt the same way." Marta moved into Stewart's way.

He was trapped. He couldn't just be rude. That would be too noticeable. He turned to look at her and about dropped his full glass of wine. "Yeah. Not my style, either. Excuse me. I need a glass of wine." He headed toward the waiter. His mind was in overdrive. Damn. That woman's necklace looks just like my bracelet. I might have to follow her. Maybe if I had a matched set, I could triple my money. Then, I'd really be rich.

"That's odd. He had a full glass in his hand. Ian's right. He's jumpy." Marta spoke softly to herself. Looking at her watch, she figured Bart and Clark to have been gone at least a half an hour. Sitting down on a soft, cream colored, leather chair, she figured she might as well watch everyone. Some new people had entered and were talking to a striking woman by the door. Marta was just close enough to hear most of their conversation, some of it alarming.

"I'm sure Bart will be back any minute. I believe he has a new client, and they are finalizing a deal. You know how these art collectors are. They think and think and think. Then, they want everything done right now." The tall, brunette laughed, and they all moved toward the far wall.

Just as Marta was wondering what to do next, Bart and Clark entered the room from the hidden doorway and made their way to Marta. With a big smile on her face, Marta stood up and kissed Clark on the cheek. "Darling, we have dinner reservations. Remember?"

Bart took her hand. "I'm sorry. It was my fault I kept him so long. But, it was worth it. Right?" His gaze lingered on her necklace.

Clark put a huge grin on his face. "Marta, my dear. I have just found a Picasso I can't live without. Bart here is fantastic. In fact, his man will deliver it to me tomorrow. Then I can have it shipped home. We truly have something to celebrate tonight." He slipped his arm around Marta, bringing her closer to him. "Now, Bart, we really must get to dinner, or Marta will never forgive me."

"I understand. I hope you enjoyed looking at my gallery of art, Marta. It would please me if you would come again some time. In fact, I would love to see your necklace up-close. All fine things are of interest to me." Once more he stared just a little too long at Marta's necklace, and his smile seemed forced as he turned to Clark. "It has been such a pleasure doing business with you, Clark. Please let me know when you would like to add another piece to your collection. I have contacts all over the world. Now, I must visit with my other guests before they think I deserted them. I believe you can find your way out." He led them toward the doorway.

Clark and Marta bid goodbye and headed down the stairs. The two oversized guards opened the doors, never uttering a word. Stewart watched the couple exit.

Chapter 49

Ian was waiting for them in the water taxi, where they boarded and headed across the canal. Marta looked around. "Boy, am I glad to get out of there. Where are we going?"

Ian navigated through the other boats. "We're going to meet Sam and Tomas. And, in case we are followed, we really are heading to a restaurant. It's owned by Tomas' cousin, and he has the entire back room saved for us. We'll all debrief when we get there. Enjoy the ride for now."

About twenty minutes later, they were seated in the back room, sipping some Prosecco and waiting for Tomas. When he arrived, Ian took the lead. "Clark, let's start with you. Tell us what, if anything, you found out. Marta, you can fill in when he's done. Okay?"

Clark recounted his chat with Bart and mentioned going into his private, climate-controlled chamber. "This is where he keeps his most recent acquisitions, according to him. The thing is, he had over a dozen supposedly new acquisitions. That's a lot, even for a serious collector. I didn't have any chance to examine them or even see them very closely. From what I could see though, they're good if they're forgeries. He did show me the Picasso, because that's what I told him I was interested in. He let me inspect it and showed me the provenance. Unless you looked at them in a lab, they had every indication of being real."

"How long were you able to look at them?"

"For about 15 minutes or so, Tomas. I told him I was really anxious to have this new Picasso because a rival collector in San Diego said he was looking for one as well. I made him think I would do most anything to beat the other collector. So, me not examining it closely wouldn't be a red flag to him. The bad news is, I wasn't able to get any photos. He was watching me like a hawk most of the time."

"No worries. When do you get the Picasso?"

"Like we planned, I gave him a check as a down payment, Ian. He's going to have his man deliver it to Marta's tomorrow. That's when I have to give him a certified check for the remainder. I told him my bank in San Diego was closed, and I could visit with them in the morning. I also told him I was leaving in two days. He can check up on me tonight and find everything is as I said. How long after that will it take for your lab to authenticate it, Tomas?"

"It shouldn't take too long, because we have a good idea of what we're looking for based on the Picasso forgeries we have in the lab. Probably a week or less."

Marta looked at Ian. "Ian does that mean Clark has to stay out of sight for that long? He told Bart he was going back to San Diego in two days."

Clark spoke up. "I thought about that, and if I should run into him, I'll just say my plans changed. I can always say I got a lead on another painting and postponed my trip home. He thinks of me as a rabid collector anyway. Now, Marta, please fill us all in on what you did while I was in Bart's private chamber."

"Of course. First of all, Bart gave me the creeps. He kept staring at my necklace and even made an invitation for me to come back so he could look at it closer. It wasn't my imagination; he looked at it like he wanted it. Really wanted it . . . not just admired it.

"Other than that, I have boring news and interesting news. First the boring stuff. Lots of people making small talk; 'where does he get his money', 'this villa is so overdone; it's disgusting', 'who's his latest squeeze' and things like that. One comment was disturbing. A tall, gray haired man was talking to a very striking woman. At first, I thought she was a hostess for Bart as she was welcoming newcomers to the party while Bart and Clark were gone. But, the man told her to be careful around Bart. When she laughed and waved her hand in the air, the man told her he meant it. Then, he asked her if she knew what happened to Bart's last girl-friend. She walked away from him, and I didn't hear any more.

"That's when I looked around and saw the man you were following, Ian."

"Stewart Jones? What was he doing there?"

"Yes, him. He didn't appear to be looking at any art. I tried to start a conversation about a painting, but he almost jumped out of his skin and then told me he had to get a glass of wine. The thing is, he already had one in his hand."

"So, what else did he do?"

"Nothing. He just kind of wandered around the room, mostly along the edges. He didn't go out of his way to run into people. In fact, he looked like he was avoiding people."

"Okay. Clark and Marta, first impressions of Bart."

Marta spoke first. "Creepy. Too friendly, fake friendly. And, the party was fake friendly as well. I can't put my finger on it, other than it didn't seem genuine on any level. Something bothered me about the whole place."

Clark nodded. "Definitely fake, all the way around. Within minutes I was his best friend. He wanted to sell me a painting. Real bad. I don't know if he needs the money or if he's always like that. And, he was cocky. He has something I don't. In his back room, he made references to being a superior collector and again cocky when he showed me his newest treasures.

"Oh, another thing. He got upset when I said I might have more Picasso's than he does. He didn't show it overtly, but it was there. He was definitely upset."

"Right. I noticed that, too, Clark. He almost clenched his jaws when you said that."

"Okay. Thanks. Tomas, as soon as Clark has the painting we need you to work your magic with it ASAP. Sam, any news on the bracelet?"

"Yes. I talked to the curator at the museum. We have a match."

Marta gasped. "Oh my."

Chapter 50

Stewart was glad the stupid party was over, and he was back at his hotel. He had a message from Pedro telling him his boss wanted to make sure he had the right worth placed on the bracelet before he gave him any more money. Pedro made it sound like Stewart would be receiving quite a bit of money. He smiled and thought out loud. "Well, another day's wait would be worth it, especially if the money is that big." He touched the wad from Bart in his pocket. "I need to find out where the woman lives and relieve her of that necklace. Maybe I'll sit in the hotel bar and treat myself to a nice bottle of wine."

Just as he was leaving his room, his cell phone rang. "What does he want now? I just left there less than an hour ago." He answered it on his way to the bar.

"Hey there, Bart. Nice pa . . ."

Typical of Bart, he interrupted and barked out some orders. Stewart tried to interject, but couldn't even mutter until Bart stopped demanding. "Yeah. I hear ya. You want me to deliver some painting a guy bought tonight. Sure. I got the address. Wrote it down while you were talking. I'll pick it up at 10 tomorrow morning. What? Yeah. Got it. I bring the cashier's check directly back to you. Yeah. That's cool. No, I'm not in a hurry. Just wanted some space of my own. Sure, it's great working with you. I'll see . . ."

Bart had hung up. Stewart looked at the silent phone. "Damn that guy. I really need to get far away from him. I don't trust him at all anymore. I overheard some people at the party talking about his former girlfriend and what happened to her. I need to get outta here as soon as possible. One more errand for him, and I'm taking my bracelet money and splitting." Stewart was so upset he was talking to himself and pacing in the hallway just off the elevator. He almost ran into the concierge when he turned and rounded the corner to the bar.

"Good evening, sir. You seem a little upset. May I be of any assistance?"

Stewart shook his head. "No. Thanks. Just had a crummy phone call, that's all." He kept walking.

"I'm sorry to hear that. Is there anything I can do?" The concierge turned and walked along side Stewart.

"No. I just want to be alone." Stewart wondered why the guy kept walking with him.

"Alright. Tell you what, let me order a nice glass of wine for you. That might take your mind off your phone call."

"Thanks. But that isn't necessary." The guy wouldn't go away.

"I insist. We want our guests to be happy." The concierge ordered a glass of wine, showed Stewart to a table on the back terrace, and told him if he needed anything to come to him. Then he left.

"Thank goodness he's gone."

The concierge walked out, called Ian, and related what had just happened.

$\mathcal{C}$hapter 51

Ian put his phone back in his pocket and related what the concierge had to say to the group. "I think Stewart is upset about something. That was the hotel concierge. He caught him talking to himself, and he sounded pissed."

"Well, it wasn't about the bracelet. Pedro left him a message telling him it was worth a great deal of money, and the valuation would be finished in a couple of days. So, was it about the party?" Sam looked around at the group.

"No idea. But, let's coordinate our plans for the next two days. I'm going to visit with my people at Interpol and then the Venice police. The issues of the Picasso and the bracelet are somehow related, as Stewart is involved in both. I want things to happen in the right order. I'll be in touch with everyone tomorrow. Any questions?" Ian looked at the group.

With everyone in agreement, dinner was finished, and Marta and Clark were on their way back to her villa. They had taken a vaporetto to a stop close by and were now walking down a side street and over a small canal bridge. Marta was about to ask Clark if he thought George and her grandma were somehow related when Clark let go of her hand, grabbed her face and kissed her. At the same time, he whispered in her ear. "We're being followed. We're going to keep walking past your place and head to the bar around the corner and down the canal. Don't look around and don't say anything. Okay?"

He moved away, took Marta's hand, and loudly said, "Darling, I think a drink is an excellent idea. Let's see what this place has to offer." With that, he ushered Marta into the bar as he stooped to pick up a speck off the cobblestone walkway. In doing so, he had a good look at the follower, now in the shadows of a nearby building. It was Stewart.

Once inside the bar, they both ordered a glass of grappa. "Clark, who was following us?"

"Stewart. I picked up the fact that someone was following us when we stepped off the vaporetto. At first, I thought it may be coincidence as a lot of people got off the same stop we did. But, once we headed down the first side street and across the small canal, I knew we had someone back there. I wonder if Bart has him following us."

"But, why? Do you think Bart suspects something?"

"He shouldn't. Everything is in order as far as credentials and money go. But, Stewart was at the party and now this. Something's off. Let's finish our drinks and see if he's still around. You have a good alarm at your villa, so I'm not worried about him breaking in. Ready?"

Exiting the bar, Stewart was nowhere to be seen, and they headed to Marta's. Shadow greeted them with meows and purrs as they made their way up to the first floor. Clark called Ian to let him know what Stewart was up to.

"Marta, Ian wants to wait a couple of days to pick up Stewart. Now that we know he's involved with Bart, there may be something more to come of this. Both of us need to keep watch for him when we're out and about. We also need to let each other know if we're doing something alone. Okay?"

"Sure. But, do you really think he'd do something stupid? It seems like he wanted the money from the bracelet. Speaking of the bracelet, I can't wait to see it again. Sam was confident it's a direct match to Grandma's jewels. I'm so excited about it and at the same time so sad George isn't here to share it with me. What's going to happen to it?"

Chapter 52

Back in his hotel room Stewart paced, restless. "I've got to have that necklace. If the bracelet is worth as much as Pedro's boss says it is, the necklace would make it at least three times more. I need to figure out where she lives. It should be easy to grab it when she's not around. These old places don't have much for security, anyway.

"But, I have to make some stupid delivery for Bart tomorrow. Maybe he'll know where she lives. After all, she came to his party." Having verbalized his plan, Stewart felt better. He was anxious to get out of Venice and away from Bart for good.

From the lobby, Ian had watched Stewart enter, wondering what he was up to. His phone buzzed. "Clark, hello. Oh really? Well, I just saw him come in a few minutes ago. I wondered where he had been and what he had been doing. Why do you suppose he was following you and Marta? Okay. Be careful. Everything in place for the exchange of the painting tomorrow morning? Great.

Ian left the lobby and had just entered his room when the phone in his room rang. Picking it up, the same mechanical sounding voice as before gave a similar message. "She's going to get hurt unless you stop him." Then silence.

"Damn. This is disturbing." He made some phone calls; to Interpol, to Clark, to the FBI, and to the hotel manager on the outside chance they had a system where he could trace the call or at least figure out the origin. They didn't. Clark voiced the same concerns Ian was having.

"Ian, do you think the caller is talking about Marta. Or, should we be concerned about Suzie in San Francisco?"

"I really don't know. If I had to guess, it's probably one of them, though. We need to make every effort to keep them both safe. Will you call the SFPD and tell them about the call? Either they can talk to Suzie or you can. But, I'd like to have some protection with her at all times. At least for a few days, until we wrap up the Bart thing and the bracelet. Okay? As for Marta, you guys are together most of the time. Just watch your six."

"Will do. I'll call Officer Street right now. I also know a couple, both retired FBI. They'll either stay with Suzie or hang close for as long as we need them to. And, Marta and I will be extra careful. Are you going to be around in the morning when the painting is delivered?"

"Yeah. I thought I'd be sitting somewhere so I can watch. Just a second. Hold on and let me get the door." About two minutes later Ian was back. "I wonder who is delivering your painting. It probably won't be Bart."

"No. He said he'd have his man deliver it, and that means one of this hired thugs, most likely. We'll have to let him inside, and that bothers me a little. Have you or Interpol come up with anything more on Bart?" Clark could hear Ian rustling some paper in the background.

"Good timing. I just received a file; special delivery from our headquarters here."

"You guys send things through the mail? Really?"

"Well, it isn't ordinary mail. This is our own special delivery service. Whoa. This file is all about Bart. You and Marta may have been onto something when you wondered if he was connected to your murder victim in San Francisco. I need to read this, and I'll call you in the morning before your delivery."

"Do you want me to come there?"

"No. Let's not chance anyone seeing us together. I'll read it, and if I need to, I'll call you later tonight. Otherwise, first thing in the morning."

Chapter 53

Clark hung up and made a call to Officer Street. Then, he called and introduced his retired FBI friends in San Francisco to Suzie, explaining about the phone calls Ian had received. With all arrangements in place, he told Marta about the call. "I don't know if the caller is talking about you or not. It's weird, though. Only two calls and both to Ian, who hasn't really been publicly involved in any of this. It's almost like someone knows something we don't."

"I know. And, it's like they're doing a favor by warning us. To me, it doesn't really sound like a threat. Does it to you?"

"It does sound more like a warning, especially this one. But, why? And, if the caller really intended to warn Ian, why not say who is in danger. Why not give more information? And, again, why Ian and not me? I don't get it, but we have to take it seriously, Marta."

"Right. You're sure Suzie is safe? I'd hate to think of her having another injury after all she's been through."

"She's safe with her escorts. In fact, they invited her to their place in Monterey for a week. It's right on the water and built like a fortress. No worries there. I'll check in with her later this week."

"That's fantastic. Now, switching subjects . . . we have the delivery tomorrow. Are you going to let him come in or meet him downstairs? Can we go over the details once more?"

"We have to let him bring the painting up here. It would be a huge red flag if I didn't inspect it. I'm supposed to be eccentric but not stupid. And, I need to make a big deal out of giving him the check. I know he'll report back to Bart, and we want it to fit with the persona Bart saw tonight. I would like you to be in the room, watching him. Any impression you have might be helpful. We have no idea who is delivering it and how they relate to Bart. It will probably be one of his thugs. If that's the case, he will be armed, and I've thought about that as well. I'll have my weapon on me. Where is yours?"

Marta had taken shooting lessons after last year when she was attacked two different times by a thief who wanted her grandmother's jewels. Both times she fought the thief off, but suffered emotional and physical trauma. Now, after working with a therapist, a martial arts instructor, and a shooting instructor, she had decided she wanted her own handgun and had a small Ruger custom made for her.

"I keep it in the drawer in my room. Do you think I should have it here in the living room while the delivery man is here?"

"Yeah, I do. I'd like you to have it loaded and in a place close to where you are standing or sitting. I'd also like your phone to be in a pocket, unseen. Please put Ian on speed dial, so you can get him with just one button. He's going to be outside, and we aren't going to lock the door once the delivery guy comes in.

"I've also been thinking about how I need to react when I see the painting, and I've decided I'm going to get excited, giddy almost. I'm going to talk to myself a bunch about the painting. I'd like the deliveryman to become impatient but not pissed. You could egg me on, tell me I should spend some more of my moldy money and get a matched set, or something like that. We want all this reported to Bart. Maybe if he thinks he can sell another painting fairly quickly, he'll make a mistake. I know the paintings he showed to me in his vault, so I'm going to need one painted by someone other than those artists. If everything he has are fakes, he'll have to have one created in short order if he wants the sale. So, anything we can do to make him slip up, the better. Okay?"

"Got it. I can become persuasive about spending your money! Am I supposed to know anything about art and artists?"

"Not really. It's probably better if the deliveryman thinks you don't have a clue about art. Then he won't have to worry about you or report anything about you back to Bart."

"Got it. Let's go to bed. I can hardly keep my eyes open." At the mention of bed, Shadow purred and led the way upstairs.

Chapter 54

Well before dawn, the phone in Ian's room rang again. By now, he was expecting to hear another warning, and he wasn't disappointed. He didn't even try to say hello; he just picked up the receiver.

"He's closing in on her. Trust me. I know this man. He'll do anything to get it." Then silence.

Ian put down the receiver. "Well. The messages are getting longer but certainly not any clearer. I still have no idea what the hell is going on. And, that bugs me." Ian got out of bed and started making notes. Often, when he wrote things down, they made sense. So far, these did not. He started pacing and muttering.

"So, apparently some guy wants some thing that some woman has. No clue about any of those facts. I'm beginning to think it's not the lady in San Francisco. She doesn't have anything. She never had the bracelet or any paintings, either. So, it has to be Marta. And, it almost has to be associated with the bracelet. The caller probably isn't talking about Stewart. He already had the bracelet and wants to sell it. Marta said Bart really looked at her necklace like he wanted it. It could be him. But, how does he know about the bracelet? If, indeed, all this relates to the bracelet. Damn."

He sat down at the desk, picked up the file on Bart, and continued his reading from last night. "I can see why he's wanted in connection with forgeries. I'd bet a boatload of money the Picasso he sold Clark is a fake. The question remains, who is the forger? He's good, whoever he is." He spent the next two hours reading and taking notes.

"Clark and I need to talk. Maybe we won't pick up Stewart just yet. I'll see if Tomas can speed things up with the Picasso, and we can wrap this up next week. Now, it's time for a shower, and then I need to position myself in the vicinity of Marta's villa before the delivery."

Clark and Marta were discussing where Clark would inspect the painting once the deliveryman arrived. "Marta, I want you to stay back a little after you bring him up here. But, be sure to make comments. I don't know if the guy will be smart enough to remember everything you say, but I want him to remember that I might be persuaded to purchase another painting. Okay?"

"Got it. I really would like to have all of this finished. In fact, I . . ." Clark's phone rang, and he looked at the screen.

"It's Officer Street with the SFPD. I'm going to put him on speakerphone. "Officer Street, I have you on speaker as Marta is here with me. What can we do for you?"

"Clark, Marta, we talked to Dr. Clyde Janssen. We believe your opinions about him are correct. There is something going on with him. He was extremely nervous the whole time we were talking. We have no cause to arrest him, and he isn't even a person of interest at this time. We just wanted you know what we discovered." Officer Street paused.

"I believe you found out from Mr. Hanson's attorney that his former partner was Bart Astor. Well, there is no record of any Bart Astor existing anywhere, ever."

"Officer Street, that's what George's journal made reference to; it was like the guy disappeared off the face of the earth. Were you able to find out anything about their business or the patents they had as a partnership?"

"Nothing."

"So, what's up? Who is this guy?"

"We don't know yet. Our guys are having a hard time locating anything that connects Mr. Hanson to a Bart Astor. Like you said, it's like he vanished. Or, never existed. What we do know is that Dr. Clyde Janssen's wife's maiden name was Astor."

"Whoa. That's too coincidental for me. Where's the wife? Can you pick her up for questioning?"

"Well, Clark. That's the problem. Close to two years ago she was killed in a car accident when her car ran off the road along the coast, north of The City. It's still listed as an open investigation as there were marks on her car leading the investigators to believe she was run off the road, and therefore it wasn't an accident. She died in that accident."

"Why didn't Clyde tell us, Clark?"

"Marta, I have no idea. Officer Street, did Clyde mention this to you, or how did you find out?"

"No. He never mentioned it. That, in itself, was odd. This only surfaced recently when we looked at his past."

"Have you asked him about her or the accident?"

"Not yet. We wanted you to know. We'll let you know what he has to say. And, like I said, he's not a person of interest yet. The last name Astor is fairly common, so there could be no connection to Bart Astor at all."

"Yeah. I don't believe that. Do you?"

"It's kind of hard not to have some questions about the name. We'll get back to you."

Marta and Clark were still discussing the information Officer Street had given them about Clyde and his wife when the doorbell rang. "Okay, Marta. Showtime. Are you ready? I'll stay up here, and you can bring the man up. That way we'll have a better vantage point, in case he tries something."

She nodded and went down the first flight to answer the door. Shock registered on her face as she opened the door and looked at the man standing there with a large crate on a cart.

Chapter 55

Stewart couldn't believe his luck and thought to himself, this was going to be easier than he planned. He smiled at the small woman answering the door. Yep, easy. His lucky day.

"Hello. May I help you?" Recovering quickly, Marta looked at the cart.

"Yeah. I'm here to deliver a painting to someone, and I need to pick up a check for it. Is the painting for you? Where do you want it?" Stewart looked Marta up and down, making her uncomfortable. "Hey. Aren't you the lady with the pretty necklace from the party?"

"I do believe we saw each other at the party last night. What did you think of all the art? Did you enjoy yourself?" Speaking louder than her normal voice, Marta was making small talk, in hopes Clark could hear them and realize it was Stewart making the delivery. She also hoped Ian was outside and saw Stewart come to her door.

As she was talking, Stewart was looking around the entryway, up the stairs, and back to Marta. "Nice place you got here. Want me to take this upstairs? Do you have the check I'm supposed to pick up? I gotta get it and get going."

Marta turned only slightly to look up the stairs and that was all Stewart needed. He shoved the cart into the street, slammed the door, pulled his handgun from his belt, and grabbed for Marta. "I think I'll take the necklace instead of the check." As Marta spun out of his grasp, she slipped on the first step and landed on the floor. Things unfolded in slow motion.

Clark appeared at the top of the stairs and fired over her at Stewart. She heard the front door open and another shot; this one closer. Turning toward the door, Marta saw Ian, handgun raised. Stewart now lay on the floor by her feet, not moving. Both men rushed to her side.

"Are you okay, Marta?" Ian felt for a pulse on Stewart, who was now bleeding all over the marble entryway. Clark helped her up as she hung onto him.

"I'm fine. Just dazed. And, confused."

Ian was on the phone talking to someone. Clark helped Marta as they made their way upstairs. "Let's wait until Ian comes up and then compare notes. Are you sure you're okay? You're not hit, are you?"

Nodding, Marta sat down and picked up Shadow, who was hiding around the corner. He settled in her lap, purring. They could hear Ian finish his phone call as he came up the stairs. "The Venice police will be here shortly to take the body. Interpol is sending another agent here as well, and Tomas is coming to get the painting. Everything is going to be kept quiet for now. Bart will get suspicious at some point when Stewart doesn't return with the check and may even call you, Clark. We need to work on how that will play out. Let's talk about what happened, and then we can answer questions from the police. Marta, are you okay? Can you tell us what happened on your end?"

"Sure." Taking a breath, Marta recounted the events to Clark and Ian. "It was a shock seeing him at the door. We talked about what to do if one of Bart's thugs brought the painting, but not Stewart, so I didn't expect him at all. When I asked him if I could help him, he asked me where I wanted the painting, and he talked about picking up a check. It seemed like he was rushed. He still had the cart in the doorway, and the door was partially open. Then, he started looking at me. Really intense and very uncomfortable for me. It's like it dawned on him that he remembered me. Oh,

I know. He asked if I was the lady with the pretty necklace from the party. I tried to talk about the party in hopes that you, Clark, would hear him and realize it was Stewart and not someone else.

"That's when I glanced at the stairs. He mentioned the necklace again, saying something like he would take it instead of the check. Then, he tried to grab me. I sort of saw him out of the corner of my eye and moved out of his grasp. Only, I didn't quite manage to get away from him. I tripped and ended up on the floor. You know the rest."

"Do you think he realized the stones in your necklace match the bracelet or did he just like it because it was pretty?" Clark was sitting next to Marta.

"I'll bet he recognized it and thought he could sell it with the bracelet. He already knew he was getting a fair amount of money from Sam for the bracelet. Why not get more? I'm not sure he's just a dumb thief. Or was, a dumb thief." Ian sat down across from Clark. "Let's talk about Bart."

The doorbell rang and Ian stood up. "I'll get it. It's probably either Interpol or the police."

Chapter 56

It turns out it was the Interpol agent, two investigators with the Venice police, and Tomas. Questions were asked and answered; Stewart was identified, and his body was taken to the morgue. Tomas took the painting to the Interpol lab. Ian cleaned up the ground floor once everyone had left as Marta called Sam to let him know what had happened. Clark called Officer Street, first to tell him about Stewart and then to ask if they knew anything more about Clyde's wife.

They all came into Marta's living room about the same time. Ian spoke first. "We definitely need to put our plan in place. I'm surprised Bart hasn't called you yet, Clark. I think it's time you call him."

"Agreed. I've been thinking about what I should say. Obviously, I'm going to tell him I don't have the Picasso yet and accuse him or his man of stealing it. I'll be quite upset about that. He'll have to believe Stewart took it and disappeared when he can't find him. I don't see him getting suspicious of me. I'll ask if he has called the authorities or if he wants me to do that. That should make him a little nervous.

"I'm also going to tell him I'm going to be around for a few more days if he wants to make amends with me. Since I'm still adding to my collection, I don't want to go home empty-handed.

I don't believe I saw anything by van Gogh in the room where he keeps his extra paintings or newest collection pieces. That might get under his skin as well. And, it would cause him to be a little careless if he or his forger had to hurry."

"Good thought. We need him to make a mistake. Soon."

Clark's second phone rang; the one he used as Clark Morris. "This is probably him, as no one else has this number. Okay. Here goes." Clark nodded to Ian and Marta and answered his phone.

"This is Clark Morris. Yes, I was just about to call you since it's well past the appointed time for my delivery. What do you mean, you haven't heard from him? Where the hell is my Picasso? You don't know? How can that be? You only sent one guy to deliver a valuable painting? I expect a better answer than that. I also expect to do business with a more reputable dealer." Clark was nodding.

"Uh huh. I understand, but that doesn't help me any, now does it? His disappearance is your problem, unless you'd like me to call the authorities. I'd be happy to do that. He has my Picasso, after all. Maybe I should call them to report it missing. What? Yeah, I can wait to call them. But, see the thing is . . . I'm going back to San Diego, and I need to have a new painting with me. It's important for a lot of reasons." Clark was smiling at Ian and Marta.

"What can you do to help me? I'll tell you. I have a meeting with another collector in Milan who was getting a van Gogh for me. You got anything like that? You do? I didn't see any in your vault. Oh, I see. You have a brand new one that just came in. Well, hot dog. When can I see it? Not for a couple of days? I thought you just said you had it. Okay. I understand. I will try to postpone my trip home but I need some assurance you've got what I want. I need to let the guy in Milan know, and I need to take care of some other business if I'm not going home tomorrow." Ian had written a note and handed it to Clark.

"Hey, Bart, just to be clear . . . you have this van Gogh, right? I don't want to give up my meeting in Milan unless I know you have what I need. Any way I can see it or something? No. No. I understand. I'm just impatient, and I really need a van Gogh. Okay, send me a photo. I'll hold you to that. But, just so you know . . . if I don't have it by next Tuesday, I'm going to have to call the police about my disappearing Picasso. It just isn't right to have your guy run off with it. Yeah, sure. I know.

"Marta and me? I don't know about that. She's pretty busy, and I'm not sure how long she's staying. I'll have to ask her and get back to you. Okay? Yeah. I know. Thanks for the call. If it were me, I'd be calling the police next. Okay. Talk to you later." Clark hung up. Ian and Marta were watching him.

Chapter 57

"Well, you probably got the gist of most of the conversation. He doesn't want me to call the police; he's somewhat concerned about his guy disappearing; he says he has a van Gogh, but I don't believe that for a minute; and he wants you and me to come to dinner at his place, Marta. Oh, he'll have the van Gogh ready for me on Tuesday."

"Dinner? No way. I'm not going near that guy. He gives me the creeps. We don't have to go, do we?"

"Not at all. You'll be really freaked out when I tell you what else he said."

"What did he say?"

"He invited you and me to dinner at his place and then told me to have you wear the necklace you had on the night of his party."

"What? I know he wanted to see it. Do you think he'd do something stupid, like try to steal it from me? Is that why Stewart mentioned it? Or aren't those related?"

"That's what I'm worried about. He seems like a ruthless man who gets what he goes after. And, he's after your necklace. I can see him offering you a great deal of money for it. If he doesn't get it, I can see him trying to get it any way he can. It's a game to him. No, we aren't going to go to dinner with him. Ian, any thoughts on the conversation from your perspective?"

"Just a couple of things. If I were him and an expensive painting just disappeared with one of my employees, I'd be calling the cops. But, since he's not, it lends more credibility to our theory that it's a fake. He wouldn't want to get into any of that with the police.

"Second, how the hell is he going to get a van Gogh painted by his forger in four days? The guy must be good. Didn't he say he was going to email you a photo?"

"Yes he did. I should have it shortly. If I don't, it would be a good idea for me to bug him. What else, Ian?"

"He didn't even ask you what van Gogh you wanted. Which tells me he must have various fakes in different stages of completion. Right? Lastly, you are exactly correct in assuming he wants Marta's necklace. I never did have a chance to fill you in on the file we have on him."

"You have a file on him? For what?" Marta looked at Ian.

"Yeah. Interpol has a file on him, and it was delivered to me late last night. I just started to get into it early this morning. Our friend Bart has quite the history. I've got it with me. Let me get it."

Ian went to get his jacket and folder he had laid on Marta's counter. "I was using these as my disguise. Just a guy reading a paper, sitting at a sidewalk café."

Clark's phone, his real one, rang. "It's Officer Street again. Maybe he found out something more. I'll let him know he's on speaker. Hello, Officer Street. I've got Marta and Ian here, and you're on speaker. Is that okay?"

"Sure. They need to hear this, too. I have some disturbing news."

Chapter 58

Bart hung up from talking to Clark. "Damn. Where the hell is Stewart? It would be just like him to make off with the painting. But, if he thinks he can outwit me and sell the damn thing, he'll be in for a real surprise. I'll give him another hour and then call him again. He's not smart enough to get far." He sighed. "Now, I've got to get a van Gogh done in two days if I'm going to deliver it to Clark in four. I need to email him a photo of some van Gogh. I don't really think he'll care what it looks like. He's just another blowhard art collector with more money than knowledge."

He smiled to himself. "And, I'm going to relieve him of a lot of that money. First, though, I need to make another call. I haven't heard anything from my guy for a couple of days, and that's not acceptable. He's supposed to find the drawings and the bracelet and check in with me. What the hell do these people think I pay them for, anyway?"

Placing his call, it went right to voicemail. "Well, that's not going to fly. Apparently, he needs to be reminded he doesn't mess with me." Bart made another call.

"That's what I said. Here's the address. Take care of the problem, but don't kill him. I need him alive. If you screw up, you'll wish you were dead." Abruptly ending the call, Bart took a deep breath. "Okay. Time to quit messing with imbeciles and make some art."

Chapter 59

"We're all listening. What's going on?" Clark spoke to Officer Street.

"Well, we've been looking into the death of Dr. Clyde Janssen's wife. When it happened about a year and a half ago, it was first logged as an accident. Dr. Janssen was understandably upset at the time. A few months after the accident, homicide got involved, and Dr. Janssen didn't want any investigation. He was adamant it was just a freak accident. Kind of odd to the officers at the time, but everyone grieves differently, so they moved on. There were a lot of things going on right then in The City, and their time and efforts were better spent on investigations where they were needed. It's a red flag now, but not at the time.

"Anyway, fast forward to last week when we went back to Dr. Janssen's condo to ask him some more questions. First of all, he wasn't there. Not too strange . . . other than we had just talked to him, and he said he would be home. We waited about an hour and called him again. Right to voicemail. So, we called his work number and were told Dr. Janssen quit the day before. He no longer works there."

Clark looked at Ian. "What? Why would he do that? Did he move to a different department?"

"Nope. He's gone. They even have him off the personnel list. So, we call him again. No answer. Back to his condo and this time we meet a neighbor in the courtyard. Says he knows Clyde quite well. Then he says Clyde left for a sabbatical and was going to be gone several months. When we asked if he knew where Clyde was going, he shook his head."

"Okay. But why quit at Stanford? Especially when he knows we're looking into George's death, and he was such a good friend of George." Marta looked puzzled.

"Right, Marta. There's more. This neighbor, Fred, asked why we were looking for Clyde, and we told him we needed to talk to him about a missing person. Didn't want to get into all the details. So, Fred tells us he has a key to Clyde's condo, and we could look around his condo if we want. Maybe we could find where he went."

Clark smiled. "Don't you just love friendly neighbors? What did you find? I'm assuming it's not good."

"Right, again, Clark. We really weren't sure what we'd find, but it wasn't what we were most afraid of. When we walked in with Fred, the place was neat as a pin. But, here's the deal, his personal items were gone. No clothes in the closet to speak of. No laptop computer, no books or files, no personal items in the bathroom, no phone or computer chargers . . . nothing personal was there. It was like no one really lived there."

Marta spoke again. "Was this the first time you were there? Maybe it always looks like this."

"No. We were there one other time, and both of us distinctly remember things that were now missing. Plus, Fred knew he had books and files filling one whole bookcase that was now empty."

Ian spoke to the whole group. "So, could he really be on a sabbatical?"

"We don't think so. He never mentioned it to his office at Stanford. We asked after Fred told us that. It's not adding up, and it's not making sense. We wanted you to know."

"Thanks. You know, both Marta and I thought he was odd, too nervous at times, and he almost seemed like he knew more than he was telling us. But, George must have trusted him, because he left him some money and his home in his will. Do you suppose that's where he is? I'm sure you've talked to George's attorney."

"Officer Casey just got off the phone with him before we called you. The attorney and Dr. Janssen talked a couple of days ago, and Dr. Janssen was excited about both the money and the house. Nothing in the conversation between the attorney and Dr. Janssen was off, according to the attorney. And, apparently Dr. Janssen never mentioned a sabbatical to the attorney, either.

"We had also told Dr. Janssen not to leave, as the murder investigation of Mr. Hanson was ongoing. He had kind of joked at the time and told us he had no place to go anyway. Something's not right."

"Yeah, Officer Street. We all agree. Something's going on. By the way, did the car accident ever get reopened?"

"Yes. That's the second thing I was going to mention. The investigators reopened it shortly after we first questioned Dr. Janssen. There are several disturbing pieces. She definitely did not drive off the cliff by herself. The entire side of her car has paint from another vehicle, like she was forced off the road. And, her brakes were not working. The fluid had all been drained out by a hole they found in the brake line."

Ian and Clark nodded in unison.

"There's more."

Chapter 60

Working in his private, concealed studio Bart finished the van Gogh in record time. "It's not my best work, but he's not going to know the difference. He didn't even ask the right questions about art the other night. And, never once did he ask for a provenance. Probably doesn't even know what one is. He just wants to have more paintings than his friends in San Diego. This is an easy sale and good money. Better than the Picasso for sure.

"Speaking of the Picasso, I still haven't heard from Stewart or from my man in the States." Bart dialed Stewart again, and it went right to voicemail. "That weasel. He will be sorry. He can't hide forever."

His second call was answered immediately. "Mr. Possa, I just got back from his condo. He's not there but I have a lead on where he is. I'll find him and report back. Give me another day."

"Okay. One more day, but no more. Did you find any jewelry, specifically a bracelet, or any drawings?"

"Nope. Nothing like that at all. Place was kind of clean."

"What do you mean, clean?"

"Clean. Empty. Like he was in the process of moving out. Things that should have been there, weren't. But, he left a clue. I'll find him."

"You'd better." Bart ended the call.

"Time to decide how much I want for the van Gogh. I'm going to tell him I had to call in a favor and make it sound like I had to work hard and do some deals to get it. I'll figure out some story he'll believe and call him tomorrow. Tell him the deal is in process.

"But, now I need to sit and think about the drawings. I really need those, especially since he's dead. I wonder what the old coot did with them. Too bad Franco didn't get him to talk before he shot him. For that matter, what did he do with the bracelet? I'd bet a lot of money it matches the necklace Marta was wearing. Wonder where she got that? I swear they're both part of those royal jewels I'm supposed to have. Too bad Clark declined my dinner invitation. Now I'm going to have to figure out another way to get it. Stewart would have been the perfect one to break in to her villa while she's out. Where is that rat, anyway?" Looking back at the van Gogh, he smiled. "God, I'm good. I deserve to have it all."

Muttering to himself as he left his studio, "I've got to have it all. He didn't deserve any of it."

Chapter 61

"Officer Street, we're listening. What more do you have?" Ian spoke first.

"We have an investigator looking into everything connected to Dr. Clyde Janssen as he is now both a person of interest and a missing person. One red flag, and it's a major one. His bank account grows regularly, by fairly large amounts."

"Okay. You've got our attention." Clark looked at Ian. They both had some ugly thoughts running around in their minds. They'd seen this type of scenario before.

"From what we found, deposits varying from $25,000 to $50,000 have been made off and on for the last two years. All in his account. All cashier checks."

"Were you able to trace the cashier checks?"

"Ian, they came from an offshore bank account in the Cayman Islands. The trail is cold after that, as you know how hard it is to get any more information than that."

"When did the deposits start?"

"Here's what we have so far. The first deposit of $50,000 was made a few months before his wife went off the cliff. Then, nothing for a little while. Three months after the accident a deposit of $25,000 was made, another $25,000 two months after that. Then, a space of about a month and a half before three more deposits of

$35,000 each were made each about a month apart. Then another space. Finally, the last deposit was made the day before Mr. Hanson was murdered. Coincidence? Ian and Clark . . . I'm sure you don't think so. It's all got to be connected."

"So, what's the SFPD's take on all of this?"

"Clark, we now have the FBI working on it, and we're helping them. Mr. Hanson's murder is considered closed because of the murder of Franco, but his murder is still an open case. The theft of the bracelet and paintings are still open as well. We're working on those. The FBI is involved because of Dr. Janssen's bank account and the fact that he's missing. As you know, together those two incidents represent more than just a missing person's case.

"Clark, I know you have Suzie Thomas in a safe place. Can you keep her there for another week or so?"

"No problem. I'll make a call."

"Thanks."

Ian spoke up. "What's the next step? Do you think Dr. Janssen's disappearance is connected in any manner to Mr. Hanson, the missing paintings, the bracelet, or anything here in Italy?"

"We aren't positive and don't have all the pieces connected yet. But, it sure looks that way. Dr. Janssen seems to be the common denominator in all of this. Did you find the paintings stolen from Mr. Hanson?"

"Officer Street, we have not found George's paintings. But, the Interpol office here has some others that are a match to those." Ian filled him in on what was at the lab in Venice, what was happening with the bracelet, and finally the fact that Stewart was dead.

"I've asked Interpol and the Italian police to send a copy of everything to you as he was wanted for questioning in a murder in San Francisco. You should have that soon. We're pretty sure he was the one who shot Franco, because of the bracelet. Now, we'll need to decide what happens to it."

"Thanks, Ian. I've got to go. We have a briefing in a few minutes on Dr. Janssen. When I know more, I'll call."

*C*hapter 62

Clark, Ian, and Marta all wore the same look. Clark spoke first. "Wow. Marta and I thought something was off about Clyde, but this is bizarre. Disappearing, telling his neighbor he was going to be gone for a long time, and the money."

"There's no way he was making that kind of money from Stanford, is there?"

"No, Ian. Not at all. It's kind of like he was either selling something on the side or doing something that wasn't legit."

"But, what about his wife and the accident?"

"Marta, good question. And, why didn't he ever mention her to us. I know we weren't friends, but wouldn't you think it would at least come up in conversation?"

Ian nodded. "Okay, guys, let's concentrate first on Bart, the bracelet, the stolen paintings, Stewart, and the van Gogh you're supposed to get. Let's wait for SFPD to connect the dots with Janssen. First, the bracelet. We know Stewart had it, probably stole it from Franco and most likely came across it by accident when he killed Franco. We also know he was anxious for the money. We have to assume Bart didn't know about the bracelet. Was Stewart going to split once he had the money from Sam?

"Now Stewart. What happens when Bart finds out Stewart is no longer around? We can hold off any information about his death only for a couple of days. We know he worked for Bart, he delivered the paintings from Mr. Hanson's house to him, then showed up at the party doing whatever, and now he delivered the Picasso. But, did he do anything else? He's just a small time guy. Bart probably uses him for the dirty work when he doesn't want to send one of his thugs that guards his door."

"Ian, maybe we should leak his death to Bart. That might cause him to do something."

"Good thought, Clark. Let's go over information from the rest of the file we have on him. Interpol wants him for questioning in some art forgeries and thefts in various places. Our investigators are positive he's involved, but whenever we've been close to pinning something on him, he either disappears or our informant does. Now, with the Picasso, we'll have a better chance. If it's a fake, we can question him for that. But, he'll have an excuse or something. He always does. I'll bet there are no fingerprints, and it's still not the proof we need. With the van Gogh, you will need to ask some specific questions and tape his answers. You have more knowledge of art and can come up with questions to trap him. You can play dumb or whatever you think will work, Clark."

Marta had been listening and thinking. "Guys, something is still bothering me about Bart and his concentration on my necklace. Stewart also wanted it. But, why?"

"Well, Stewart probably wanted it to sell. I can't see him wanting it for anything but money. Bart, on the other hand was interested in it when we were at the party, Marta. Why? Just because he liked it; someone else had it, and he didn't? Or, is it more than that? And, if it is something more, how do we find out without putting you in danger?"

"Well, there was one section in our file about him and some jewel thefts. But, those were several years ago. Maybe he's trying to get back into that business. Who knows? For now, let's concentrate on the Picasso and think about the rest. I've got to get to the lab. Clark, you and Marta should go talk to Sam about the bracelet and see if he's found out anything more about its history. It's getting late, and we should all meet back here tomorrow morning."

*C*hapter 63

The following morning all four were sitting in Marta's kitchen. Sam had joined them with the bracelet.

Ian took a drink of coffee. "I'm sure we all have more information. But, first I need to tell you I had another warning call last night. Same mechanical voice, but a longer and more informative message. This one said, and I quote, "He's mad and getting madder. Stop him now before he kills again. I know Marta is his intended target. He won't have me for his snitch anymore. I'm taking care of that. Be very careful. Signing off.""

"Wow. The caller has to be talking about Bart. Right, Ian? And, to mention Marta specifically. Any idea who the caller is? And, what does he mean when he says he's signing off?"

"No idea, Clark. We just have to stay vigilant and keep you safe, Marta. Let's recap what we all know about anything connected to Bart. Sam, why don't you start with what you know about the bracelet? Have you been brought up to speed on the events?"

"Yes, I have. Thanks. Okay, the bracelet. The museum curator was able to fill me in on some more history. She had been continuing to research Marta's grandmother's family, as it was of interest to her. Like we already knew, she discovered another document listing several pieces of jewelry, coins, gemstones, and other artifacts all associated with that royal family. Some of it Marta already has. Some of it we aren't sure where it is or if it even exists anymore.

"She talked to this jeweler who knew a goldsmith who knew an artist who knew another jeweler. One person's great-grandparent was the best friend of another person's uncle . . . and so on. The amazing thing is, everyone had good notes and receipts. Back then, it was not only important you were the royal family's jeweler. But, it was also important you were the supplier of the gemstones or the gold used by the royal family's jeweler. Everyone's name or shop was on everything. Which makes it easier for her to complete the cycle. Apparently, though, no one person or journal or log had listed where it all was or how it became divided up. She had to contact multiple sources.

"The bottom line is, this is one of the bracelets in the premier set. That set includes pieces we already have: the tiara and large necklace, both worn for official events, and the bejeweled letter opener, a special piece for the ruling lady. The missing pieces include a smaller necklace, worn every day, a pair of matched bracelets, and a stickpin one would have used in a collar or on a lapel. Like I mentioned, we now have one of the bracelets. No idea about the rest."

Marta was excited. "This means we have more information about Grandma's family. But, Sam, did the curator have any idea why George's grandma had the bracelet?"

"No, Marta, she did not. So many of the surnames did not include the woman's previous or maiden name. That makes it hard to follow. Her best guess is one of two things. His grandmother was related to your grandmother, which would make sense why he has it. Or, his grandmother was a favorite servant of your grandmother or someone in her family, which would mean it was a gift. She has found nothing to support either of those, however. I'm not sure we'll ever know."

"Sam, that is fantastic. What happens to it now?"

"Marta, that's up to Interpol, the FBI, or other law enforcement. Will the owner's family want it? We have no solid proof it belongs to you, although history says it does."

Ian spoke up. "Sam, Clark tells me there are no family members, and Mr. Hanson's will does not list it. I will intervene with Interpol and suggest it go to Marta. Marta, will that be okay?"

"Absolutely. I think it should be on loan to the museum where the tiara and necklace are. Sam?"

"I agree. They are fantastic pieces, and that way they can be seen by many people. Italy thanks you, Marta."

"Okay. I think that puts closure on the bracelet. I'm going to fill you all in on what the lab has discovered about your Picasso, Clark."

Ian relayed the findings from the lab. "It is a definite match to the other Picasso in our lab. Paints, canvas, brush strokes all match. And, they aren't Picasso's work. The lab is one hundred percent certain of the match. Interestingly, there are no fingerprints on it anywhere. None. If it was a legitimate piece of artwork, curators and other handlers would have worn gloves, but there would be prints from Picasso or someone who might have carelessly handled it. There is nothing. That's one red flag.

"Second, the paint is easy to chip off the canvas. Again, legitimate artwork wouldn't do that. Having said that, the paint dates to recent times. Not Picasso's timeframe.

"Third, the signature isn't quite right. To a casual observer and even a fairly serious collector, it passes for the real deal. But, up close the swirls on the S are just a little off. You really have to look at these. And, I doubt he was selling to curators or that level of collectors who would take the time to inspect every detail. It's more likely he was selling to casual art collectors and those who wanted to get a steal on a Picasso.

"So, what does this mean? It means we could bring him in for questioning. Like we said before, though, he'll have an excuse, a high priced attorney, and we'll just make him a little more cautious for next time. It won't do us any good. We need more. Clark, have you heard from him about your van Gogh?"

"Not yet. I was going to call him and act a little jumpy about the painting. Tell him I heard some things from his friend, Stewart. I figured that would get him to act careless. He's got to be wondering where Stewart is by now. But, in the long run, will that do any good? Or, will it just cause him to stop for a while? How do you want to proceed, Ian?"

Clark's phone rang. "It's Officer Street again. Let's see what the SFPD has found. Hello, Officer Street. I've got you on speaker again. Ian and Marta are here, along with Sam, our jeweler contact. What's up?"

"It's about Dr. Janssen."

Chapter 64

"What the hell do you mean, dead? I specifically told you not to kill him. This is not acceptable." Bart was shouting into the phone.

"Bart. Hold on. I didn't kill him. I'm just hearing this from my contact at the police station. When I was at this condo the first time, I grabbed an address from a sheet of paper on the floor. That turned out to be an office building in the Financial District. With no office number or name, he could have been going to anyone there. So, I left and was just about back at his condo to stake it out when my contact called me and said they had a body at his condo's location. When I got there, the cops were all over so I waited a block away. Next thing I know, the medical van pulls up. They all go inside, and I can't really tell what's going on. An hour or so later, they all leave. My contact confirmed it was him.

"No idea what happened. What do you want me to do, Bart?"

"Stay low and stay in contact with your source. I need to know what happened. See if you can get back in the condo to find anything of interest concerning the drawings or the jewelry. Call me with any new information." Bart hung up and slammed his fist onto the desk.

"Damn. Things are getting worse. What the hell would he have done with his plans? Why is this so difficult?

"And, where the hell is Stewart? Why can't we find him? Time to call in another favor."

Chapter 65

Everyone looked at each other and Clark answered. "We're all listening, Officer Street. Did you find him?"

There was a long pause. "Officer Street, are you still there?"

"Yeah, I'm here. It's just been a rough morning, that's all. And, we have an FBI agent here that knows you, Clark. Tom Peterson said to tell you hello. He's now the lead investigator here. But, he told me I could fill you in since he's busy."

"Tom's a good guy and will be an asset to you. Tell him hi. Now, what's going on?" Clark looked at Ian with a puzzled look.

"Okay. I'll back up a little. Remember I told you we went to Dr. Janssen's condo, and it looked like he was moving out? Well, our investigators did some more digging into his past, his bank account, and his work at the lab at Stanford. When we talked to a colleague at Stanford, he mentioned Dr. Janssen told him he needed to disappear because things were getting too stressful. The colleague joked and said they were all stressed out lately. That was last week. Then, this week he disappears.

"So, we were planning on going back to his condo to search it even more thoroughly when a call came in from the same neighbor we talked to earlier. He said he heard a strange noise coming from Dr. Janssen's condo. The place is well built, and they usually don't hear anything from the other units, but this one bothered him for some reason. The neighbor was concerned, especially when we had just been there and the place was so clean. Officer Casey and I met Tom and his partner there. What we found wasn't good.

"Dr. Janssen had been shot. It was a self-inflicted gunshot wound, according to the medical examiner."

"What?" Ian and Clark looked at each other.

"I know. Hard to believe. He was sitting in a chair, the weapon on the floor. The ME puts the time of death consistent with the noise the neighbor heard. Now, this is why the FBI is taking the lead. He left a note. More like a long letter. You're not going to believe what he says."

"We're listening. What does he say?"

"I'm going to email you the letter so you can all read it together. The gist is he was being blackmailed, it relates to Mr. Hanson, and some other guy he calls The Bastard. We're still digging into it but Tom wanted me to send it to you. He has a bunch of questions for you, Clark, and Ian. But, you need to see it first. He's going to call you in an hour. I've got to get to a briefing. The letter is on its way.

"I'll have to catch you later."

Clark disconnected the call. "What the hell is going on?" His other phone, the one he used with Bart, rang, and he ignored it.

Chapter 66

Bart hung up, more disgusted than before. "What the hell is wrong with everybody? Don't they know who I am?"

He had placed a call to one of his thugs who had been looking for Stewart and wasn't happy with the answers. "Mr. Bart, it's like he disappeared. Poof. Vanished. We've exhausted all our resources, and he's nowhere to be found. We even checked with the police. Nothing. There's no point in continuing to look. He's gone." The thug had hung up before Bart could lay into him.

"Those jerks. Who do they think they're messing with? They don't tell me when the search is finished. I might just have to show them who's the boss. And, what do they mean . . . he's vanished? You can't just vanish. Unless you're me, of course." His snarl turned into a wicked laugh.

Bart's second call had gone no better. His contact in the States didn't answer. Then, he placed a call to Clark Morris to tell him his van Gogh was ready. He was going to insist they meet over drinks, and he was going to get the necklace from Marta, one way or another. But, that call went right to voicemail as well.

"This is ridiculous. No one ignores me and gets away with it. Maybe Mr. Clark Morris and his girlfriend, Marta, will just have to have an accident. That would show them." Pleased with himself,

Bart sat down to think about what type of accident he could inflict on them.

Giggling to himself, he clapped his hands. "It's simple. They have to die. Too bad for them. And, I know just how. This is going to be fun. And, then it will all be mine."

Chapter 67

Clark printed out four copies of the emailed letter. It wasn't long, but full of information, accusations, and speculations. It was also a little confusing:

To Whom This May Concern:

By now, you know I'm dead. I can only hope the authorities are reading this and not anyone else. I liked George. I really liked George and had no idea the bastard was going to kill him. I wish I could have been more help to the police and Clark in finding George's drawings. They've got to be in his house. He wouldn't have let them out of his sight. I know George would have done everything he could to keep them from him. Everything. Especially after he tried to steal the jewelry from George.

George knew he was a bad guy and was going to come after everything else George had. George also knew he was quite mad, becoming madder, and he was concerned about what he was going to do next. That's why George kept tabs on him all these years. And, now I understand who George was talking about when he told me the rat would take the bait. George was close to having absolute proof he could take to the police.

I'm positive George's keys were what we found in his paintings. The bastard wouldn't have been able to figure that out. George was protecting his inventions. George loved puzzles and I believe this was just one of his many puzzles. He probably wanted the bastard to steal them. I also know for certain the bastard was the one who ran my wife off the road. I always suspected it, but now I have proof of that, too.

Let me start at the beginning. I was the one who saw the bastard trying to drug George and steal his jewelry and plans. I was in another room at George's house, and I didn't think the bastard saw me until he showed up at my office and threatened me. He said he would kill George and my wife if I didn't help him. He only wanted information. I saw no way out at the time.

For a while I told him what George was working on, copied a couple of plans for him, and hated every minute of it. Then I stopped and was about to go to the police when he killed my wife. He upped my payments but also upped the threats to George.

I felt stuck. So, I did some more dirty work for the bastard. Only, he was never satisfied. He wanted everything George was working on, and I finally quit giving it to him. Then he killed George. And, probably tried to kill the cleaning woman and who knows who else. He's after Marta because she has something he wants. I think it's jewelry and may be related to George's bracelet. Tell her to be careful.

But I know I'm next. He will kill me if I let him. I tried to find George's drawings so I could give them to someone else but I have no idea where they are. Somehow George knew the bastard was selling fake medical device plans and forged paintings. I'm positive that's why George had those two forgeries. I think George thought the bastard forged them. I know I'm rambling but I feel like I don't have much time.

Someone needs to find the bastard and put him away for good. He's slippery, and I think he has a contact in the police department. One time he told me it wouldn't do any good for me to go to the police because his man would tell him if I had been there. I've been leaving warnings with Clark's friend, but have no idea if they're going through.

I hope George and my wife didn't die for nothing. The bastard has to be caught. Maybe this will help. He lives in Italy. He doesn't use his real name. The bastard goes by Bart Possa. He was my wife's uncle. Please put him away. I wish this could have ended differently.

I'm sorry.

Chapter 68

There was silence as they all read the letter. Then, Ian whistled. Marta sighed. Clark looked at everyone. "Whew. What a mess. We have to believe most of this is true. I know the FBI will get to the bottom of it in San Francisco. Ian, what will Interpol do about Bart here? Do we have to let the Italian police take him in? Or is this enough to get to him?"

"I'm not sure. I have to make a couple of phone calls to see if the FBI has contacted us yet."

"Speaking of phone calls, I let one from Bart go to voicemail. Let's listen to it now. Oh, it looks like I have two from him."

Putting the voicemail calls on speaker, they heard Bart report to Clark in the first one. "Mr. Morris, Clark, I was fortunate enough to track down a van Gogh. Had to pay a little more than I wanted but I won't pass that cost on to you. I'm just glad to be of service. I will have it here tomorrow and could deliver it to you then. Do you want it delivered to the same address as before? Just let me know. I can't wait to see if there's something else I can do for you. Call me as soon as you can. Ciao."

"Well that was fast. Could he have had that painted or painted it himself that quickly?" Ian was looking at Clark.

"It's possible, or he already had one finished. Hopefully, he thinks I'm just a dumb, eccentric collector and not a real art collector that would take time looking at it. Let's listen to the second call."

"Clark. I'm extremely disappointed I haven't heard from you. Do you still want the van Gogh? It's imperative I know as soon as possible. I'm going to have to go out of town for an extended period and need to deliver it this evening. One of my guards and I will personally bring it to the same address at seven o'clock this evening. Please be advised I will expect a certified check when it is delivered. We will wrap up our transaction at that time. Call me immediately upon receipt of this message."

Ian chuckled. "He sounds pissed. Not even a good bye or a Ciao at the end. Maybe he is getting concerned. And, he's going out of town. What's up with that? Wow."

"Well, if we are to believe Clyde's letter, this is the former partner of George. He's a forger and a scoundrel."

"Don't forget bastard, Clark." Sam smiled.

"Right. And, it all fits. I'm just not sure if he's really going out of town or is in a hurry to get some money. He's hard to read. He's a slick one. At any rate, we need to be prepared to be here tonight. I'll take possession of the van Gogh and give him the check. Ian, you've got a couple of hours to figure out how Interpol wants to handle the rest."

"I need to make some calls and visit with headquarters. I'll be back in an hour or less."

Sam stood up at the same time. "What do you want me to do?"

"Can you stay here with Marta and me? You can stay out of sight but it wouldn't hurt to have another set of eyes and ears on the whole transaction."

"Will do. My shop is closed today anyway."

"Good. Let's form a plan for the three of us. We can let Ian know when he gets back."

Chapter 69

Bart made a call to his favorite thug. "I've got a job for you. It's an easy one. There's a guy expecting a delivery tonight at seven. He thinks it's going to be a painting, and he thinks I'm going to be delivering it. All you have to do is show up a little late, kill both the guy and the lady he's staying with, and break some things. Make it look like a robbery. I want only one thing from the place." He described the necklace to his hired thug.

"Got it? Oh, and make sure no one hears you. Use that fancy new silencer. I'm going to be eating dinner and then sound asleep with my latest squeeze as an alibi. After you bring me the necklace, you get paid double the normal rate. Then, disappear for a while. Any questions?"

He hung up and called the woman from the party, inviting her to dinner at his place. He thought to himself, this is too easy. He called a chef and asked for dinner to be delivered at 7:30. He planned on adding a sleep additive to her after dinner drink. She'd be fine in the morning, but wouldn't remember much about the night. She'd never see him again.

He looked around his studio. "I won't be needing the van Gogh for a while. I'll just hang on to it for later use." Sitting down at his desk, he made a few notes as he went over everything in his mind. Muttering to himself, "The plan is in place. I can't believe how easy that was. People are so stupid. But, I have a problem in San Francisco. There's one loose end, and I don't like loose ends. I might have to send someone from here over there to finish that job. These guys are much more efficient."

Chapter 70

Clark, Marta, and Sam finished discussing their plan. "This time, Marta, you're not answering the door. Bart said he was delivering it, but I don't believe that for a minute. He'll have one of his armed guards deliver it, and we are not going to give him a chance to do something stupid. We have to assume Bart doesn't know we're on to him, but at the same time we have to be prepared for anything.

"This is how I want events to happen."

Ian called to let them know he would be delayed. Interpol was working with the FBI in the States and the head of Italian security in Rome. The Venice police were also involved. They had one plan to arrest Bart if he showed up at Marta's with the fake van Gogh. If he didn't, they had another plan to arrest him at his villa. Everything was being carefully coordinated given the short notice. "Clark, be careful. I'm not sure when I will be there, but you won't see me when I do arrive. We also don't want any obvious police presence outside Marta's, because we don't want to alert Bart or his men. At the same time, we're concerned about Marta. If any shots are fired, we don't want her to be in their path."

"Ian, we were just talking about that and have a plan. Marta is not going to answer the door. Sam just informed us he trained with the Italian Special Forces as a civilian. Since his shop deals with high-end jewelry and millions of Euros, he wanted to be prepared.

Maybe a little overkill, if you ask me. But, hey, it sure helps us now. He's going to answer the door. And, he will be armed. It will be obvious to the person with the painting, regardless of who it is, that Sam has a weapon. I'll be waiting at the top of the stairs and Marta from another room. We will all be armed, again obvious to the delivery person. We're betting it won't be Bart. I can't believe he'd stoop so low as to do any delivery work. It will be one of the thugs we saw at his home."

"Good idea on all of it. I've got to get to a meeting with Interpol now. I hope to be there by seven or eight at the latest. There will be two special agents outside somewhere by seven. Take care and stay safe."

Marta had been reading Clyde's letter again and had some questions. "Okay. Bart and George were partners. Right? But, we still don't know what their falling out was initially about. Clyde mentions Bart was stealing George's ideas, and George had mentioned that as well. Right? Was the split before or after that? I guess at this point, it really doesn't matter. Then, somehow Clyde enters the picture, and his wife is Bart's niece. I wonder how all that happened. Again, probably doesn't matter.

"Clyde mentions he saw Bart try to poison George and steal his drawings. Bart somehow knew Clyde was there and saw him, so he blackmails Clyde using death threats on his wife and George. Clyde must have been really scared of Bart not to go to the police. Ultimately, Bart wanted George's plans and some jewelry, according to Clyde. He also mentions Bart was selling fake plans and fake paintings. George must have found out and was setting a trap. Is that what he was doing in the wine cellar when he was shot, I wonder? Is that why he had the forged Monet's? Did he know Bart was forging paintings?

"The jewelry must be the bracelet. But, why say jewelry instead of bracelet? Is there more? The police said the chest was empty, so where is more jewelry? Do you suppose it's hidden with the plans? There are so many unanswered questions."

"Marta, you are right on. We'll probably never know all the answers. Right now Interpol is working on all the forgeries connected with him. I know Ian, and I know they are forming a plan to not only arrest Bart, but to put him away for a long time. Clyde also mentions a contact in the police department. I'm assuming it's the SFPD, and I'm glad Tom is working that end in San Francisco. If Bart is that devious, he probably has more than one contact.

"For now, we need to concentrate on our plan. Everybody comfortable? It's almost seven. Let's take our places and wait. I'm going up to your top floor, Marta. I can see real well in one direction, but I have no idea where he will come from. Maybe I'll catch a glimpse of any special agents as well. Okay with both of you?"

Sam and Marta both nodded and took their appointed places; Sam on the ground floor, positioned by the front door and Marta in the kitchen on the first floor. Sam had one weapon in his hand and another visible in a shoulder holster. Marta was out of sight, behind the edge of the refrigerator, also with her handgun. Once Clark checked the street from the third floor window, he settled down in the first floor living room, handgun in his right hand.

Chapter 71

"Do you suppose he's not coming, Clark? It's about a quarter to eight." Marta sat down in the kitchen.

"I think he's showing me who is in charge by being late. I also think he wants me to call him and be upset. Then, in his mind, he has the upper hand. Clyde mentioned something about Bart becoming madder. I wonder what all that was about? He's a scoundrel, untrustworthy, and egotistic. Maybe underneath, he's crazy, too."

Clark called downstairs to Sam. "You doing okay, Sam?"

"Doing fine. I'm mentally preparing my role and waiting patiently. You and Marta okay?"

Just as Clark was going to answer Sam, the doorbell rang. As they planned, Sam waited and in a few seconds, it rang again. Stepping to the side in the darkened entryway, Sam flipped the switch to turn on the outside light, and unlocked the front door, making more than normal noise. As he reached to open the door, it burst open and a lone figure dressed from head to toe in black crouched down and entered. From behind the door Sam noticed the weapon in his hand had a silencer. The gunman turned toward Sam in the dark and fired once. Then he looked up the dark entryway toward the first floor.

When Clark heard what he thought was a silenced shot, he quietly moved out of the living room and around the corner. Silently and deliberately, the thug crept up the marble steps toward Clark and Marta, never making a sound. Clark wasn't sure how far up the stairs he had come. He motioned for Marta to move into the dining area around the corner. Sam hadn't made a sound. They waited.

The thug reached the top step and paused. At the same time he pulled a knife from his pocket. The chandelier hanging above him suddenly lit up the entire entryway and a split second later several gunshots echoed in the quiet. All hit their mark, and the thug tumbled down the stairs. From above Clark called out. "Sam, check for a vest."

"Already did. Didn't do him any good, though. He's dead."

The front door flew open as two men, weapons drawn, entered Marta's villa. "Special Agents. Don't shoot."

Sam put down his weapon and identified himself. Clark called out from upstairs. "I'm FBI and my weapon is on the floor." He stepped into view, his empty hands held out for the agents to see.

Satisfied everyone was who they said they were, the Special Agents radioed for help in taking care of the body. Ian came through the door. "Sorry I'm late. Apparently, I missed all the action. Fill me in."

Sam explained the events from his end. "His shot missed me as he aimed at the blanket we hung over here as a decoy. I waited in the dark while he went up the stairs, and when he was almost at the top I turned on the light, which spooked him. I had a clear shot and fired four times. Clark knew I was taking the first shots and would fire only on my command. Two shots hit his vest and one hit his arm; the one that killed him hit his neck."

"Obviously, he was here to kill. Both Marta and Clark? Most likely given the weapons on him. Why didn't he have the painting or didn't he care about looking legit? Clark, do you recognize him?"

"I do. He was one of the doormen at the party. So, we know he works for Bart. But, what we don't know is why Bart wanted us dead. Did something give him reason to disbelieve our story?"

"I'm not sure. Maybe Bart had word of Clyde's death in San Francisco and was starting to connect the dots. Or, maybe he really does have an inside contact who talked about one or both of you. I wonder when this guy was supposed to report back to Bart. It's getting late, so my guess is either by a coded text or tomorrow morning. We were going to pick Bart up for questioning in the morning based on the findings from the lab on the Picasso. I'm thinking we need to up that to tonight. Catch him off guard."

"I agree, Ian. I wouldn't wait. He might be expecting a report tonight from this dude. If he doesn't get it, that would be two of his lowlifes who disappeared without reporting in. That might cause him to pack up and run."

"Yeah. I'm making a call, and then we're going to his villa. I want Marta and Sam to stay here with an agent. Clark, you can come with us. Got a vest?"

Chapter 72

An hour later, seven armed agents from various agencies stormed into the ground floor of Bart's villa. No thugs or guards met them at the door. The faint smell of gunpowder lingered in the stairway. Ian, in the lead, motioned for everyone to move as they scrambled up the stairs. What they saw when they entered the grand show-room turned living room on the first floor was not what they were expecting.

The attractive brunette, who acted as Bart's hostess the night of the party, sat on the floor. Her bloodstained, partially ripped dress slid off her right shoulder, and her bare feet were spread out to the side. What once was a styled upward hairdo now hung limply around her face. In her lap sat a small handgun. Slowly turning her head, she looked at the men who entered the room.

Ian and Clark, first to enter, surveyed the rest of the room. Broken dishes were scattered all over the shiny wood floor, food lay nearby, and shattered crystal wine glasses reflected the light from the overstated chandelier above.

The woman let out a small whimper.

As the other the agents cleared the rest of the villa, Clark knelt down by the woman and moved the handgun away from her. "Are you okay? Can you tell me what happened?"

She looked up at him, and he noticed a bruise beginning to form near her left eye. She nodded.

"Can you stand up? Let's get you off the floor." Clark helped her up and directed her away from the mess and the body. They sat down on a small sofa in the far corner, overlooking the Grand Canal.

"I killed him."

"Okay. Can you tell me your name?"

"My name is Sophia. I was his girlfriend. Until tonight." Sophia began to cry softly, and Clark grabbed a napkin off the table.

"Sophia, that's a start. Can you tell me more?"

Sophia nodded, blew her nose, and told Clark about the evening. "He invited me for dinner. I was so happy. We were drinking before dinner, and then he started bragging about making money from paintings and about having a special necklace. He took me in his studio to show me a van Gogh and laughed and laughed about it. It didn't look right to me, and I questioned him about where he bought it. I don't think he knew I work at a museum. He got upset and grabbed my arm and dragged me back out here. He was really rough with me and tore my dress. Then, he pushed me down into the chair and filled my wine glass. I spilled some wine, and he yelled at me. I didn't know what to do." She sniffed again and looked at Clark.

"So, I thought if I changed the subject it would help. I asked him about the necklace he mentioned. He really scared me as he told me about it. His eyes got buggy, and he started breathing real hard. It was like he was obsessed. Then, he said something about the wrong person having it, and she was going to die tonight. I told him not to talk like that, and he told me I would die, too, if I didn't do what he wanted me to do." She paused and blew her nose again.

"What did he want you to do, Sophia?"

"He wanted me to take a special pill he had in his hand. When I asked him why, he got really upset and tried to shove it in my mouth. It was on my tongue. I was really afraid of him at that point. His eyes got even spookier; his hands shook, and he was yelling. I had never seen him like this. The pill kind of slipped out of my mouth, and he hit me." She touched her cheek.

"What did the pill look like?"

"It was a small white capsule. I have no idea what it was."

"Where is it? Did you swallow it?"

"No. It's probably on the floor somewhere. Right after he hit me, I dropped my wine glass, and it broke. He called me some names, threw his wine glass at me, and the next thing I knew, he had this gun." She pointed to the handgun Clark had moved out of the way. "He pointed it at me as he grabbed my hair and yanked me up out of my chair. I heard it click. I have no idea where I got the strength to grab it from him, but I did. I probably surprised him. The gun went off, and he fell toward me. I didn't know if he was dead. I grabbed the gun, and I slid away from him. I figured I would shoot him again if he moved. Then you came in. What's going on, and who are you?"

Chapter 73

Bart's villa had been processed by Interpol, the Italian police, and the Venice police, Bart's body had been moved to the morgue, Sophia's story had been recorded, and she was back at her home, resting with a Special Agent, and everyone else gathered at Marta's villa. The complete story, as they knew it, was recounted for Sam and Marta.

"So, he wanted my necklace. Is that why the guy was here to kill us, Clark?"

"We have to assume so. That, and maybe he had some information from his San Francisco contact that was making him nervous about us. Ian, were you able to wrap up the artwork and the connections to Bart?"

"Well, we have him for all the forgeries and their sales that we know about. There are probably ones out there we'll never find, as he was pretty savvy until these last few months. He seemed to be going downhill, mentally at least. His villa will be sold, once Interpol and the Italian police are completely finished with it. He has no known heirs or relatives. I'd say Bart Possa or Bart Astor is done for. We can thank Sophia for doing us a great favor. How about San Francisco, Clark?"

Clark called Officer Street while Ian, Sam, and Marta sat out on her terrace drinking Prosecco. "Officer Street, you're on speaker, and I have everyone here."

"Hello, everyone. I have terrific news at last. First, we were able to figure out who the inside contact was that Bart was paying. Turns out he used to work for Bart and George when they had their business as a techy-type assistant. Then he came to work as a computer guy in one of our police offices downtown. Funny thing, though. He was taking money from Bart, selling him information, and reporting to him and, get this, he was also informing George about what he just sold to Bart. How he kept everything straight, it's hard to tell."

"Officer Street, this is Clark. Do you think George knew all along what Bart was doing?"

"It appears so. At least for the last few years."

Marta interrupted. "Officer Street, is this why George was in his wine cellar when he was shot? Do you think he knew the thieves would be breaking in that night?"

"Absolutely. The informant said George specifically told him to tell Bart that particular night was the best night to break in. He gave him some story about selling his house and told him to make sure Bart knew that. It's kind of confusing, but it makes some sense. I mean, we've all wondered what George was doing just sitting in his wine cellar."

"Right. And, we've wondered how Franco had the code to the alarm there. It does fit together."

"Right, Ian. Anyway, to continue. There was another break in at Clyde's condo, after we had already processed it. Thanks to another neighbor, we caught the guy in the act, and he sang like a canary. This guy had been working for Bart for years, hiring thugs and keeping an eye on both George and Clyde. The guy he hired recently was a loser by the name of Stewart Jones, according to him. Go figure! Lastly, we discovered Clyde had made a will shortly before he died."

"How did you find that out?"

"Well, Clark, the attorney called us. Clyde used the same attorney as George had, and the attorney received a letter from

Clyde, similar to the one he left in his condo. In that letter, Clyde told the attorney to call us when he received the letter. He said he would be dead if the attorney had the letter. So, he called us. Clyde left everything to Suzie. She should be finding out about this in the next few days."

"Clark, that's fantastic news for Suzie. She deserves it after all she went through."

"I agree, Marta. Now, I have to go to a briefing. Anything else on your end?"

After Officer Street hung up, Sam turned to Marta. "Marta, remember I told you the curator matched the bracelet to your grandmother's jewels and that she said there is another one and a pin? She has recently come across some more information. There is also a pair of earrings. These are not part of the royal set that were worn for special occasions, but are ones the ladies wore every day. They will have smaller stones and will not be as ornate. We still don't know where those are. But, it's good news."

"Sam, be sure to thank the curator for me if I don't have the chance. I am so excited to keep finding pieces of Grandma's history. It's like she is still here showing the pieces to me. I'm just sorry it always seems to come with ugliness, though." Marta looked at Clark.

"Marta, if you can get away I think we should head to San Francisco fairly soon and wrap up any loose ends there. Then, we can . . ." Clark's phone rang. "Well, what do you know? It's Suzie.

"Suzie, it's so good to hear from you. Did you have a good time in Monterey? Is it okay if I put you on speaker as I have Marta here with me?"

"Of course. In fact I want to talk to both of you. The attorney tells me you already know this, but I now own George's home. Isn't that fantastic? I don't really know all the details, and I'm not sure I want to, but I do understand someone that inherited it first died and left it to me. And, left me so much money. I can't believe it. When are you and Marta coming back here? I want to move in and have a party with the two of you here. Do you think you'll be here by next week?"

Chapter 74

Two weeks later Clark, Marta, and Suzie were gathered in Suzie's new home. She had spent time sorting through George's furnishings, selling some, donating some, bringing her things in, and moving other things around until it felt like her home. She had insisted Marta bring Shadow, who was now checking out every corner. The chest George had willed to Suzie sat on her nightstand. Some of his paintings with the squiggly white lines hung around the house.

After she had given them a tour, they headed to the dining room. Suzie had opened a bottle of George's wine, and they all made a toast to him.

"I can't believe everything that has happened. It seems like forever and yet it seems like yesterday. I decided to keep all of George's paintings, even though we'll never really know what his purpose was in painting them the way he did." Suzie looked at the ruby red wine in her glass. "Oh, Clark, I almost forgot. After dinner will you help me with the wine in the cellar? I have George's old spreadsheet, but I'm confused about a few bottles that aren't on there. Did you ever find out why some of it was stolen?"

"Suzie, we have no idea why he'd want George's wine." Clark took a sip. "I'd be glad to look at the wine, however and see what I can help you with."

Dinner was finished, and they each carried a glass of wine to the cellar room. Suzie put in the alarm code and asked Clark. "Do I need to keep this alarm on all the time?"

"I wouldn't think so. As long as the door is closed, you will be fine. George probably wanted to make sure his wine was safe." Clark opened the door, and Shadow darted in.

"Of course. It's a room he hasn't inspected yet, and the door was shut. That's a perfect invitation for a cat. Shadow, you don't need to be in here." Marta followed him and bent down to pick him up. He had found a pen on the floor and batted it behind a large format bottle leaning up against another bottle. Both were sitting precariously on a small box on the floor. Marta reached for Shadow at the same time Suzie reached for the first bottle. It fell onto the second bottle; they both fell off the box and crashed onto the marble floor, as Shadow made a dash for the hallway.

"Well, I'll be damned." Clark was the first to recover. "That sly old fox."

Broken wine bottles lay on the floor. No wine spilled out, however, as there was no wine in them to spill. Instead, rolled up paper filled the insides of the large bottles.

"Is that what I think it is?" Marta carefully reached for one of the rolls of paper.

"I'd bet on it." Clark was moving glass out of the way and picked up the second roll.

"What are those?" Suzie looked from Marta to Clark.

"These are George's drawings. This is where he kept them. Safe. And, probably why the lock on the door." Clark picked up a small broom from the corner and swept the glass to the side. "We will look at these on the table in a couple of minutes." He looked at two more large bottles sitting under the bottom shelf. Pulling them out, he could tell they contained no wine, either. "All these large bottles are where he kept his plans. Smart man. Who would ever think to look at these?"

"How did he get them in here?" Suzie had picked up one of the unbroken bottles.

"Look at the bottom." Marta turned another unbroken bottle upside down. "The bottom unscrews. Clever guy."

"Right. And, you wouldn't know it to look at it. It looks like a normal bottle of wine. I'm impressed."

After cleaning up the broken bottles, they took all the plans to the dining room table. Shadow had rejoined them and was sitting on Suzie's lap, purring. "Marta, Shadow was the one who found these. If he hadn't run past them, they wouldn't have fallen over and broken, and we would have never found the plans."

"At least not until you had a party and wanted to open a large bottle of wine." Clark was carefully unrolling the plans. "Look at this. George has a spreadsheet with each invention and its corresponding number, just like Clyde originally told us. The next column shows which painting goes with each invention, and the last column explains which wine bottle has which set of plans. Whoa. Talk about confusing. But, I guess he really did have a key. We just didn't know what to look for." Clark unrolled another set of plans.

"I'm not an expert on drawings, but these look like some of the ones in George's journal that Clyde was excited about. They might be for the robotic arm he mentioned. We should take these to Stanford. Someone who worked with George and Clyde will probably be able to use these."

"I can do that, if it's oaky. I am resuming my studies at Stanford and have a meeting there with my advisor tomorrow afternoon. He will know what to do with them." Suzie sighed. "I can't believe George died for these. Are they really that valuable, and did his former partner really think he could just steal them?"

"They are valuable, Suzie. But, from what we now know about Bart, he was mentally unstable and had become more unstable in the last few months. Somehow, George must have known that. Or, maybe he didn't trust him from the beginning. Who knows?" Clark stood up, and Marta picked up Shadow.

"Suzie, thanks for the lovely dinner. Clark, Shadow, and I need to get going. Let us know what Stanford says."

After they left, Suzie wandered around her new home and decided it was time to get ready for bed. Upstairs in her bedroom, she picked up George's small chest, now sitting on her nightstand. "Oh, George. How I wish things could have turned out differently. But, now I know how I'm going to use some of your money. I've decided to get a business degree and an art history degree. I want to open my own gallery. I've already signed up for private lessons, and Marta is going to work with me on understanding art from a practical level. Since I can't thank you in person . . ." She looked up. "So, I'll assume you're watching. Thank you, George."

She set the chest down, missing the edge of the nightstand, and it fell softly to the carpeted floor, the entire lid popping off.

"Oh dear. I didn't mean to break it." Picking up the pieces Suzie attempted to reattach the lid to the small hinge on the back-side. The bottom fell out. "Crap. I'm destroying it." As she picked up the padded bottom, she noticed the sparkles.

*E*pilogue

Stanford was elated to have George's drawings, crediting him and honoring him for all his inventions and drawings with a small ceremony. Suzie was honored to be a key part of that ceremony, especially since Marta and Clark were able to attend. Everything else connected to George was wrapped up.

Ian finished working with the Italian police. Bart's former clients were notified about the inaccuracy of the authenticity of their paintings, many of his hired thugs were arrested, and Interpol considered that case closed. Ian left a message for Clark as he headed for Singapore. "Clark, don't get too comfortable in San Francisco. There's a connection here I'm going to need your help with. Talk to you later."

Marta and Clark approved of what Suzie was doing with George's house, his money, and her career choice. "Suzie, George would be so proud of you."

"Thank you, Clark. That means a lot to me. Did I tell you I'm starting my lessons tomorrow? I'm putting George's studio to good use. You'll have to stop and check on my progress." Suzie touched her earrings as the trio walked outside in the sunlight.

"Those earrings look fantastic on you, Suzie." Marta watched as the small, brilliant, teal blue stones sparkled in the sun. "It's like they were made for you."

"Marta, thank you so much. I really think you ought to have them, though. Didn't they originally belong to your grandmother?"

"Probably. But, if she were alive, she'd want you to have them. For all we know, she and George may be watching and approving right now." Marta smiled and hugged Suzie. "I'm so glad you found them. They suit you. Remember George when you wear them. He'd like that."

Marta's phone buzzed and she looked at it. "I have a text from Sam. He says they found something more and can't wait for me to see it. I wonder what?"

About the Author

WENDY VANHATTEN is a published author, editor-in-chief for "Prime Time Living Magazine," wine, food, and travel editor for "WEMagazine," and travel enthusiast. She has taught writing at the college level, writing workshops, and is affiliated with Bay Area Travel Writer Organization, http://www.batw.org/.

Her children's books, the Max and Myron series, teach children to read while developing good character traits.

Travel advice and photos are updated weekly on her blog at www.travelsandescapes.blogspot.com. Her books are available online at Amazon or from her website, www.wendyvanhatten.com.

Additional Titles by Wendy VanHatten

My Life, The Sequel: A Girlfriend's Guide to Personal Success

When the Cat Speaks . . . Listen: A purr . . . fectly good way to enjoy life

Dad's Hidden Box

HIDDEN TRUTHS SERIES
Champagne Lies
Vineyard Secrets
Dark Legacy

MAX & MYRON SERIES
by Wendy VanHatten and R David Kryder
with illustrations by Corie Barloggi
    Max and Myron Learn Please and Thank You Max and
    Myron, My First Day of School
    Max and Myron I'm Sorry, Please Forgive Me Max & Myron
    Learn Please Don't Tease
    Max & Myron Learn Big and Small, Short and Tall

The Authorship Journey: A profitable adventure? by Wendy Vanhatten, Ginger Marks, Misty Taggart, and Tracee Gleichner

Available on Amazon.com and fine bookstores everywhere.

www.ingramcontent.com/pod-product-compliance
Lightning Source LLC
Chambersburg PA
CBHW020326260626
47156CB00004B/1391